LOVE BY THE BOOK

Also by Jane McBride Choate in Large Print:

The Courtship of Katie McGuire

This Large Print Book carries the
Seal of Approval of N.A.V.H.

LOVE BY THE BOOK

JANE McBRIDE CHOATE

Thorndike Press • Waterville, Maine

Published in 2002 by arrangement with Jane McBride Choate.

Thorndike Press Large Print Paperback Series.

The tree indicium is a trademark of Thorndike Press.

The text of this Large Print edition is unabridged.
Other aspects of the book may vary from the original edition.

Set in 16 pt. Plantin by Liana M. Walker.

Printed in the United States on permanent paper.

Library of Congress Cataloging-in-Publication Data

Choate, Jane McBride.
    Love by the book / Jane McBride Choate.
       p. cm.
     ISBN 0-7862-4623-5 (lg. print : sc : alk. paper)
     1. Reading teachers — Fiction. 2. Police — Fiction.
   3. Large type books. I. Title.
   PS3553.H575 L69 2002
   813′.54—dc21   2002028426

To my parents,
Bill and Georgia McBride,
who shared with me their love of reading

CHAPTER ONE

The phone shrilled insistently.

Anna grabbed for it. "Jeff, where are you?"

"Ms. Lancaster? Anna Lancaster?" an unfamiliar voice asked.

"Yes?" Impatience edged her voice and she tried to curb it. "I'm Anna Lancaster."

"This is Sergeant Lester, ma'am. Your brother —"

"Jeff! What about him? Where is he? Was he in an accident?"

"No, he wasn't in an accident. He's been arrested. He gave us your name."

"Arrested?" She let the words sink in. "For what?"

"Possession of marijuana. Can you come down to the Fifth Precinct station? And, ma'am, if you have a lawyer, it might be a good idea to bring him along."

A lawyer? Where would she get a lawyer? Especially at two o'clock in the morning.

Anna tugged on a pair of jeans, pulled a

sweater over her head, and grabbed her purse. She arrived at the station house fifteen minutes later.

She hovered at the door, unsure of where to go. Three sullen teenage boys slumped against a wall. She scanned their faces, looking for Jeff. *Where was he?*

"Would you be Ms. Lancaster, ma'am? Anna Lancaster?"

She whirled upon hearing her name and encountered a middle-aged policeman.

"Where's my brother?"

"He's this way." The small, balding officer, who didn't resemble the policemen she'd seen on television, gestured toward a hallway.

She followed him, all the while telling herself that this was a nightmare, one she'd wake up from any moment. Except that the moments had stretched into minutes, and the nightmare hadn't disappeared.

The room was bare except for a table and chair. Jeff slouched in the chair, his eyes defiant, his lips twisted into a smirk. Beneath the bravado, though, Anna detected fear. She wanted to take him in her arms, tell him everything would be all right, but knew he wouldn't welcome such a display of emotion.

"Jeff." She waited.

He gave her a cocky smile. "How ya doin', Sis?"

"How do you think I'm doing? I got a call at 2:00 A.M. telling me you'd been arrested."

He had the grace to look ashamed, if only for a moment. "Sorry."

"One of the officers said something about marijuana." *Tell me it isn't true,* she silently begged.

"I had a couple of joints on me. Cops probably planted them." Jeff sneered at the policeman, who didn't bother to respond. His bored look said he'd heard it all before.

She forced herself to take a breath, a long, slow one that kept her from saying things she'd regret later. "We need to get you out of here."

For the first time, Jeff looked at her. "Can you do that?"

She glanced at the officer, who nodded. "I think so. But first I want to know what happened." With an effort, she kept her voice steady.

"Mike and I were hanging out together. Just having some fun, you know. He got pulled over for a busted tail light. Then they ask him if he's been drinking. First thing we know, we're being dragged in here."

Mike Rafferty.

Several years older than Jeff, Mike made her feel uneasy whenever he was around. Maybe it was the way his gaze raked over her, an insolent look that made no effort to hide his contempt. She might have guessed he was a part of this.

She was about to say so when she noticed Jeff's expression. He was waiting for her to do just that. Maybe she'd surprise him for once.

She turned to the policeman. "What do we need to do to get my brother released?"

"You'll have to fill out some forms and then put up bail." He looked at her kindly. "This your first time here?"

She nodded, forcing back tears. Tears weren't going to help Jeff.

The officer put a hand on her shoulder. "Come on. I'll show you."

The formalities stretched into another hour. Anna sat in a chair, head bowed, shoulders slumped. She looked at her watch. In three hours she'd be getting ready for school. She still had papers to grade. She had a meeting with one of her students' parents tomorrow. Today, she amended. Instead, she was sitting in a police station waiting for her brother to be released from jail.

"Ms. Lancaster, you can go now. Jeff's

in your custody. He'll have to show up for trial. If he doesn't . . ." The kind-eyed officer didn't finish. He didn't have to.

"Thank you. We'll be there." She squared her shoulders and picked up her purse.

Anna bit back the questions that hovered on the tip of her tongue. *Now is not the time.* She stole a glance at her brother.

He'd dropped his defiant attitude and looked like what he was — a scared kid who was trying hard not to show it.

"Want to talk about it?" she asked as they threaded their way through the gray-walled corridors.

He shrugged. "Nothing to talk about."

"Jeff, it's 5:00 A.M. I've spent the last three hours at a police station bailing you out of jail and you tell me there's nothing to talk about?"

"It was a bad bust. The cops are out to get Mike. He had a couple of joints on him and gave 'em to me." At her gasp, he waved a hand. "It's nothing, Sis. I'm a juvie. Mike says juvies get off light. He couldn't afford to get caught with stuff on him." Jeff shrugged, elaborately casual. "No big deal."

"Jeff, you were caught with drugs in your possession." She took a calming breath.

11

"What kind of friend is this Mike Rafferty if he lets you get punished for what he did?"

Jeff's sigh was filled with ill-concealed impatience. "It's not Mike's fault. It's like I told you — they probably planted those joints in Mike's car earlier." At her disbelieving look, he flushed. "Well, it could've happened that way."

"Is that what you're going to tell your lawyer?"

"Lawyer?" Jeff looked at her, the hint of fear she'd detected earlier now full-blown. "What lawyer?"

"The one you're going to need to get you out of this mess."

The frightened look in his eyes deepened. *Good.* Maybe now he'd start to tell her the truth. Her hopes died the next moment.

His eyes shuttered and Jeff hunched a shoulder. "Look, Sis, everything's cool. Just lay off for a while, okay?"

Torn between wanting to hold him in her arms and wanting to shake some sense into him, she did neither. The tear that slipped down her cheek went unheeded. She was too tired to even wipe it away.

Brady Matthews was fed up.

12

It hadn't been a good day, it was an even lousier night, and tomorrow promised more of the same.

He studied the young woman and the sullen boy. The boy he dismissed almost immediately. The girl looked tired. Of course anyone was entitled to look tired at — he checked his watch — 5:00 A.M. Still, there was something about her, something that made him take a second look. She wasn't exceptionally pretty, not in the usual way. For one thing, she was too thin. Her clothes hung on her as though she'd recently lost weight. Her hair, a pale blonde, was scraped back from her face and tied at the nape of her neck. Her eyes were huge and dark.

It was her eyes that caught and held his attention. They betrayed her fear and exhaustion, yet he sensed something more behind them. An inner strength that told him she'd faced tragedy and survived.

He shook his head, clearing it of the fanciful notion. He didn't even know her and he was weaving an entire personality around an expression in her eyes.

A diet of junk food and not enough sleep were getting to him, he decided. Add to that two kids and a caseload that didn't quit and you had one burned-out cop.

The artificially cooled air, laced with stale smoke and sweat, did little to dispel the heat that blanketed the city, even at night, and he wiped his forehead with the back of his hand.

"Who's the girl?" he asked the desk sergeant.

The sergeant glanced up. "Anna Lancaster. Came here to pick up her kid brother. The kid was caught holding."

Brady nodded. He'd heard the same story often enough. Harried-looking parents here to pick up teenage sons or daughters.

"Poor kid," the sergeant said, voicing Brady's thoughts.

"Which one?"

"The girl. The brother's a smart mouth. Didn't even look at her when she came to get him. He was plenty glad to get out of here, though. Swaggered out like he was some kind of royalty."

"Why aren't I surprised?" Wearily, Brady pushed back his cap and wondered why anyone thought smoking pot was glamorous. More often than not it landed them in the county jail. He wouldn't wish that on anyone, much less a scared kid. Still, they were luckier than some.

His lips tightened as a picture flashed

through his mind: a girl, no more than thirteen or fourteen, stretched out on a slab in the morgue, after she'd overdosed on crack.

He'd seen it all. Contrary to popular opinion, cops didn't get used to it. If he ever started getting used to it he'd get out of the job. Quick. A cop who didn't care was dangerous — both to himself and to others.

He took one last drink of coffee long since turned bitter. "I'm pushing off."

"See you tomorrow. Make that today." The sergeant laughed at his own joke.

Brady gave the expected grin and pushed open the station door. The stale night air, heavy with pollution and heat, did nothing to improve his disposition. Time was, he mused, when a person could breathe the air. Not anymore. He tasted the staleness on his tongue.

He checked his watch. Late again. Mrs. Barney, the woman he'd hired to stay with his niece and nephew, would be waiting for him. Somehow, his promise to be home by midnight had gotten lost in the steady stream of "customers" the Fifth Precinct had processed.

He let his thoughts drift back to the girl and her brother. Chances were he'd be seeing more of the boy. That was one bet he hoped he'd lose.

After five hours of sleep, Brady was back at his desk. The phone rang and he picked it up wearily.

"Detective Matthews? This is Linda Gorsey, Jennifer's teacher."

Brady shoved a pile of papers into a drawer and closed it. "Yes, Mrs. Gorsey. What can I do for you?"

"I'd like to meet with you as soon as possible . . . about Jennifer. Could you stop by later today?"

He checked his calendar and decided it wouldn't matter if he squeezed one more appointment into an already overcrowded day. "I can be there at noon." Another skipped lunch.

"I'll be waiting."

The soft click of the phone signaled she'd hung up, but Brady continued to hold the receiver. It was probably nothing to worry about, he told himself. But he couldn't completely banish the thoughts that niggled at his mind for the rest of the morning.

Three hours later, he waded through a sea of kindergartners on their way to the cafeteria.

"Whew," he said, finding Mrs. Gorsey waiting outside the fourth grade classroom.

16

"They do have that effect, don't they?" She held out her hand and led him into a classroom where he squatted into a pint-size chair.

"You may remember that I've spoken to you before about Jennifer's reading."

"I remember." He waited for what was coming.

"It's gotten worse. I've given her extra help. But it isn't enough. I've talked with Chad's teacher. He's reading better than Jennifer is, and he's only in second grade."

"I try to help her at home, but . . ."

There was never enough time for everything. Becoming a parent at age thirty-two was demanding all of his coping power, and then some.

"She needs help, Mr. Matthews. More help than I can give her. If Jennifer's problems remain untreated, they're only going to get worse."

Brady raked a hand through his hair. "Where do I get this help?" *If his sister, Leigh, were alive, she'd know what to do.* But Leigh was dead, and Jennifer and Chad were his responsibility now.

"I'd like to arrange a staffing," Mrs. Gorsey said, interrupting his thoughts.

"Staffing?"

"Where everyone involved would be

17

present. You, myself, the school psychologist, Jennifer's pediatrician, and a reading therapist. We'd share information and then decide what's to be done to help Jennifer. If you like, I can set up the staffing for sometime this week."

"Sure." *Where was he going to find the time?*

"I like Jennifer, Mr. Matthews. She's a sweet child. I hope that together we can help her."

Brady dredged up a tired smile. "I appreciate your concern."

For the first time since their meeting began, the teacher smiled. "I know it can't be easy for you, caring for two school-age children all by yourself."

You don't know the half of it, he wanted to tell her. He thanked her once more, his head still spinning with what she'd told him.

Brady pushed open the door and shaded his eyes against the noonday sun. At this altitude, the early June sun beat down with merciless energy, singeing all that it touched.

He walked slowly to his car, still thinking about Jennifer. He'd known something was wrong, but he'd attributed it to the many changes she'd faced in the last six months.

Losing her mother to cancer wasn't easy on anyone, much less a nine-year-old child.

Jennifer and Chad had already known more grief than any two children should have to endure. Their father, a firefighter, had died in an accident when Jennifer had only been three and Chad one.

At the station Brady closed the door to his office behind him, hoping for some privacy while he tried to make up his mind what to do about Jennifer.

A rap on the door signaled the end of his solitude. "Come in," he called.

"Sorry to bother you, Brady, but the lieutenant wants us to check out this address." Jim Davies, his partner, held out a warrant.

Brady checked the address: 1542 Cherry Avenue.

"What's it about?"

"The boy that lives there is suspected of pushing junk."

The kid last night and his sister? For her sake, Brady hoped he was wrong.

This part of the job never gets any easier, he thought, as he stood outside a small brick house flanked by rows of petunias. Knocking on someone's door and changing their lives. Perhaps forever.

He waited while his partner rang the

bell. When the door opened, Brady recognized her immediately. The girl from last night.

Her cheeks were flushed, her eyes bright. "Jeff . . ."

Brady watched as the expectant look on her face faded.

"I'm sorry," she said, pushing hair back from her face. "I thought you were my brother. He sometimes forgets his key."

"Anna Lancaster," Davies said. "We have reason to believe that there may be drugs on the premises. We have a search warrant."

"Sorry, Ms. Lancaster," Brady said, hoping to soften what must be a shock.

He took a moment to study her. Her eyes still wore the haunted look from the night before, but she held her head high. Her hair was loose, and wheat-colored curls tumbled about her face. How had he not thought her pretty?

She opened the door a bit further and took the warrant. "What makes you think there's anything here?" she asked after she'd read it.

"Your brother has been seen with a known pusher who uses minors to stash his stuff."

"So what if Jeff's been seen with . . . that

person? That doesn't prove he's done anything wrong."

"That pusher is selling drugs to kids," Brady said, anger at the situation sharpening his tone. "This warrant gives us the right to search your house. With or without your permission."

"Do what you have to do," she said, and stepped back.

I didn't have to come down so hard on her, he thought, and immediately frowned. Detectives didn't make personal judgments, not if they wanted to keep their badge and their sanity. Still, he couldn't help but feel sorry for the woman who stood before him. Instinctively, he knew she didn't deserve this.

"I'll take the upstairs," Jim said as he headed toward a staircase.

"Right."

Brady began a systematic search of the living room. He turned sofa cushions upside down and unzipped them from their casings. The television, bookcase, and stereo received the same attention. Finding nothing, he moved to the kitchen.

She followed him.

"Look, I know you don't want to hear this right now, but I am sorry," he said as he began poking into canisters of flour and sugar.

"You're right. I don't want to hear it," she replied.

He picked up a container of salt, spilling some onto the counter and floor. He started to clean it up.

She motioned him away. "Don't bother. I'll do it."

"Maybe you should wait in another room," he suggested, uncomfortable with her presence.

She ignored that. "What do you hope to find?"

"Marijuana."

"My brother may not choose his friends very wisely, but he'd never use drugs. Last night was a mistake. It was Mike Rafferty who had the drugs, not Jeff."

Brady flicked her a sharp glance. *So she knew Mike Rafferty.* Every cop in the precinct wanted to bring Rafferty down. He had a rap sheet a mile long. Unfortunately, he was good — very good — at what he did. He used minors to keep the cops at bay. So far, to Brady's disgust, Rafferty had gotten away with it.

"You know Rafferty?" Brady asked, careful to keep his voice casual.

"No more than I have to," she said, shuddering. "He's a creep."

Brady silently agreed with her. "But your

brother hangs out with him."

"That's going to change."

He only hoped she was right.

"Clean upstairs," Jim called.

She gave Brady a what-did-I-tell-you look. "Are you planning on trashing someone else's house now?"

Brady waited rather than answering the attack.

Faint color stained her cheeks. "Now I'm the one who's sorry. You didn't deserve that. It's been a . . . rough day."

Brady resisted the urge he felt to touch her. Not only was it unprofessional, he didn't think she'd welcome his sympathy.

"It's all right." With a rueful shrug, he turned to leave.

"Detective?"

"Yes?"

"What would have happened if you'd found something?"

"Your brother's bail would have been revoked and he'd be back in jail." He watched as her already pale face turned a fraction of a shade paler.

"Thank you," she said.

There was only the faintest tremor in her voice. He doubted she was even aware of it. He hoped not. He sensed she needed to feel in control of what was happening. He sympathized with that need, understanding the fear that came when events spiraled out of one's control.

"For what?" he asked.

"For telling me the truth."

CHAPTER TWO

Anna looked at the littered countertop. The detectives had tried to be careful, but their search had left a fine layer of flour, sugar, and salt everywhere.

Darn. Why wasn't Jeff here to defend himself? Why was she always the one who ended up cleaning up after him?

The answer wasn't hard to find. They were both acting out the habits of a lifetime. Only now Jeff was involved in something she wasn't sure she could clean up.

Drugs. The word sounded so sordid, not at all like something a reading teacher ought to be involved in.

She allowed herself a rare moment of self-pity. If only their mother hadn't died last year. If only there had been adequate insurance. If only she didn't have to work all day and most nights just so they could keep their home. If only . . .

But that kind of thinking was dangerous. It was the shadow of things that might have been. Impatiently, she shook off the mood. Feeling sorry for herself wasn't going to help. Automatically, she began sweeping up the mess.

She checked her watch once more. If Jeff didn't show up soon, she'd have to go looking for him. Not for the first time, she found herself wishing for someone to share the responsibilities.

Her thoughts strayed to the detective. He'd looked genuinely sorry about what he had to do. He also looked like he might be easy to talk to. She frowned at the direction her mind had taken. Where had that come from?

When Jeff wandered in at 11:15 P.M., she pushed aside her anger. He was seventeen years old, she reminded herself. Old enough to stay out by himself. Still, she needed to know he was all right . . . that he hadn't been in any more trouble.

"Where have you been?" she asked, careful to keep her voice neutral.

"Out."

"Out where?"

He gestured vaguely. "Just out."

"Jeff, you remember what that officer said last night. I'm responsible for you. I need to know where you are, what you're doing."

"Lay off, will you?"

"What's happened to us? You used to tell me everything."

"Yeah? Well, things are different now. I'm seventeen, not some little boy who needs his big sister to wipe his nose."

But I still need you, Anna thought. "I know. But does that mean you have to shut me out completely?"

For a moment, she thought he wanted to tell her something. But he only shrugged. "Got anything to eat around here?"

Anna looked at this boy — her brother — who was now a stranger. At six feet, he towered over her by at least six inches. His shoulders and chest had filled out during the last year, making him look older than seventeen. But it was not the physical changes that disturbed her.

"I'll fix it myself," he said and began slapping bologna on bread.

She started to pour him some milk, but he stopped her.

"Got any beer?"

"You know we don't."

"Why not?"

She ignored that and put away the milk, needing a moment to shape what she was going to say. "Two detectives showed up this afternoon. They had a search warrant." She waited, for what she wasn't sure. A reaction of some kind, she guessed.

"Yeah? Did they say what they were looking for?" Jeff asked, trying to sound nonchalant.

"Drugs."

"Why'd they look here?"

Anna tried to appear as casual as Jeff. "That's what I asked them."

"What'd they say?"

"That you'd been seen with a known pusher, someone who sells drugs to kids. Is that true, Jeff? Is Mike Rafferty selling drugs to kids?"

"So what if I know Mike?" he asked, ignoring her question. "I told you the cops have it in for him. Anyway, it's not like I'm pushing the stuff."

The anger she'd tried so hard to bury boiled over. "If you know he's selling drugs . . . Why, Jeff? Why are you even friends with a man like that?"

Jeff hooked his thumbs in the pockets of his jeans. "Because he treats me like an adult! Not like some little kid who needs his hand held by his big sister. Is that good enough for you?"

She pushed her hair back from her forehead, tired of the sparring. She wasn't getting anywhere this way. She and Jeff both needed time to cool off. "I'm going to bed. Tomorrow, we need to talk."

"Yeah, yeah, yeah." He turned his back on her.

Alone in her bedroom, Anna berated herself for how she'd handled the situation. Her good intentions had fled when faced with Jeff's contempt.

When had Jeff grown away from her? They'd always been close and had grown even more so after their mother's death. But Jeff had pulled away from her, preferring the company of his friends. She'd told herself it was normal. But when he'd started hanging around with Mike Rafferty, she couldn't help but worry.

With his long hair, pierced ears, and tough-guy attitude, he wasn't the boy she'd helped raise. He'd ignored her plea to stay in school just as he ignored most of what she said these days. Minutes dragged into hours as she wrestled with questions that had no answers.

She rarely saw him anymore, except when he came home to change clothes and to eat. A reluctant smile tugged at her lips. That was one thing that hadn't changed — Jeff's appetite. It was as big as ever.

After three hours of trying to sleep, Anna got up and dressed. She'd use the early hours of the morning to polish her presentation for the school board.

Before she left for work, she tiptoed into Jeff's room. With his hair tousled about his face he looked young and defenseless, more like the Jeff she'd always known. She pressed a kiss to his cheek and wished she had the last year back. Maybe, if she'd spent more time with him. Maybe if she'd . . .

She shook her head. Second guessing wouldn't help either of them now. She'd done the best she could. But it was cold comfort when she remembered the trouble her brother was in.

Once more, she looked at the man-child, wanting to wake him and talk — really talk — like they had in the past. But she knew that now wasn't the time. He needed sleep, and she didn't need the stress a confrontation was sure to bring. Especially not this morning, when she was to meet with the school board to ask for more funds for the literacy program.

Ten more days until school let out. She'd hoped to spend more time with Jeff, but the bail money had taken a big bite out of her savings and she needed to spend as much time with her after-school tutoring as she could.

Five hours later, Anna walked out of the school administration building, more depressed than ever. Not only had the program not received the additional funds, the existing budget had been drastically cut.

"No funds," she'd been told.

Why couldn't the school board see that money spent now would save the district thousands of dollars in remedial classes for kids who'd fall behind in years to come?

She put in four more hours with her reading classes before calling it a day.

"Jeff? Are you home?" Juggling a bag of groceries, she glanced around. Breakfast dishes littered the table; an empty carton of milk and box of cereal cluttered the counter.

With a sinking heart, she checked upstairs. *Please, let him be here.*

The silent prayer went unanswered as she found Jeff's room empty. Worry, exhaustion, and a certainty that things weren't going to improve anytime soon settled over her already depressed spirits.

"... oculomotor dysfunction," the reading specialist finished her report.

What does that mean? Brady wanted to shout in frustration. He was here for Jennifer. He'd been sitting here for the better part of the day. And he'd continue

to sit here. But he wished someone —
anyone — would speak English.

"Mr. Brady, you do understand what this
means?" the specialist asked.

"I'm not sure," he hedged.

The school psychologist, the reading
specialist, and the teacher exchanged
smiles.

"In simple terms, Jennifer isn't reading
because her eyes are sending mixed-up signals to her brain."

"Isn't there something you can do to
correct that?"

"Jennifer needs to learn how to sort out
the signals her brain is receiving. Fortu-
nately, there are teachers who are trained
to do just that."

He expelled a breath of relief. "Fine."
He saw their frowns and asked, "So what's
the problem?"

"Money, Mr. Matthews. Or the lack of it.
The school board has just ruled to cut
back special-needs programs."

"But you said there are teachers who can
help Jennifer?"

"That's right. Private teachers. But I'm
afraid finding one and financing the tutoring your niece will need is up to you."

A detective's salary didn't allow for
many extras, Brady thought. But getting

Jennifer the help she needed wasn't an "extra." He'd find the money somewhere.

"Tell me where to find a teacher who can help my niece. I'll take care of the rest."

Linda Gorsey handed him a sheet of paper.

He scanned the list of names. Anna Lancaster's name headed the list. Could it be the same woman he'd met yesterday? The name wasn't that uncommon, but she'd seemed little more than a kid herself. She couldn't be the Anna Lancaster listed here with a Master's Degree in learning disorders, could she?

"This Anna Lancaster — is she any good?"

"She's one of the best reading therapists in the city," the school psychologist said. "I've referred dozens of children to her."

Brady stood. "Thanks for your help."

At home, he studied the list again. He dialed the number. "Ms. Lancaster, this is Brady Matthews. I was told you help children who can't read. . . ."

By the end of the conversation he was frowning. Anna Lancaster knew her business. She'd been sympathetic at hearing of Jennifer's problem but completely professional as she answered his questions. She was also the woman he'd talked to yesterday. He'd recognized her voice immediately. Obviously, she hadn't recognized his.

They arranged a meeting at her home the next day. His frown deepened as he acknowledged she might *not* want to teach his niece when she found out who he was.

Telling Jennifer that she needed to spend her summer vacation taking reading lessons wasn't something he looked forward to.

"Look, honey," he said after dinner that evening as he wrapped an arm around her shoulder. "It's not as bad as all that. You'll have to spend a couple of hours each day with a teacher. That's all. And isn't it worth it, if it helps you learn to read?"

Jennifer's eyes filled with tears. "I've tried, Uncle Brady. I really have. But when I start to read something, the letters get all mixed up and nothing makes sense."

"I know, sweetheart. It's not your fault. If it's anyone's, it's mine. I should have realized you had a problem and done something about it sooner."

Jennifer threw her arms around his neck. "You've been great, Uncle Brady. Chad and me both think so. Only . . ."

"Only what?"

"We still miss Mom." He heard the tiny

hitch in her voice, the one she tried so hard to hide whenever she spoke of her mother.

"I know you do. So do I." He cleared the huskiness from his own voice. "But right now the important thing is getting you reading. Right?" He put out his hand.

Solemnly, the little girl placed her hand in his. "Right."

Again, Brady was reminded of the enormous responsibility he'd undertaken when he'd agreed to be the children's guardian. Jennifer's childlike faith had touched him. It was oddly humbling. He only hoped he deserved it.

The following day, he and Jennifer arrived a few minutes early for the scheduled appointment. He looked at the house that only two days ago he'd searched for drugs. The memory gave him a moment of uneasiness as he wondered about the wisdom of sending his niece to a place where drugs had allegedly been stashed.

Then he remembered the shock in Anna Lancaster's eyes. He'd stake his reputation that she was as honest and forthright as they came. Whatever her brother might be involved in, she had no part of it.

Right now he was more concerned with convincing her to take Jennifer. He wouldn't blame Anna if she wanted nothing to do with him, but that didn't concern Jennifer. His niece deserved the best, and he was going to see that she got it.

"C'mon, honey," he said, taking Jennifer's hand. "It's not going to get any easier."

"What if she doesn't like me?" Jennifer whispered.

"Why shouldn't she like you?" he asked. It was far more likely that Anna would throw him out on sight, but he kept his thoughts to himself. He had to calm Jennifer's fears. "You're pretty, intelligent, and make a mean chocolate cake. If your new teacher doesn't believe it, tell her to ask me." Jennifer giggled.

He rang the doorbell and waited. Anna's reaction didn't disappoint him.

"You!"

Brady didn't try to feign surprise. "Ms. Lancaster, this is my niece, Jennifer."

Anna offered her hand, which Jennifer shyly accepted.

"Jennifer, there're some cookies on the kitchen table," Anna said, gesturing down a hall. "Would you like to have some while your uncle and I talk for a few minutes?"

Jennifer's face brightened and she scampered in the direction Anna had indicated.

Anna placed her palms on her hips.

"What kind of trick are you trying to play, *Detective* Matthews?"

Her emphasis wasn't lost on Brady. "No trick. Jennifer needs your help. As I said yesterday, you were highly recommended." He showed her the list of names with hers at the top.

"And you expect me to believe it's just a coincidence that after you were here two days ago to search my home, you show up again?"

He flinched at the sarcasm in her voice. He didn't blame her. Under the circumstances, he'd be suspicious too.

"I know it's asking a lot, but that's just what it is — a coincidence."

"Just how naive do you think I am?" Her raised eyebrow told him he'd have to do better than that.

"I don't think you're naive at all. Believe me, I'm no happier about this than you are."

She pointed to the list. "There are other names here."

"I was told you were the best." He handed her the file the teachers had put together about Jennifer.

Anna scanned the papers. He saw the growing interest on her face and felt his hopes rise.

She gave them back to him. "I'm sorry, Detective Matthews. I don't think this would work."

"You don't think you can help Jennifer?"

She shook her head. "I'm sure I can. I only meant you and me working together. I don't think it's a good idea."

He heard the regret in her voice. It sounded genuine.

"Because of your brother?"

She nodded. "I could recommend someone else if you'd like."

"I want you."

Saying the words aloud made him realize they were true. There was something about her, something in the way she'd looked at Jennifer, that told him she cared about her students. He wanted that kind of caring for his niece.

"What makes you think I'd want to work with you — after what you and your partner did? It took me hours to clean up the mess you made."

Instinctively, he knew she referred to more than spilled sugar and salt. "I thought you were interested in helping children learn to read. Obviously, I was mistaken."

"I *do* want to help your niece. It's just that —"

"Uncle Brady?" Jennifer, still holding a cookie, wandered into the hallway and looked at him uncertainly.

"In a minute, honey." He looked at Anna. "Will you help us?"

"Don't you like me?" Jennifer asked, addressing the question to Anna.

Anna looked at Jennifer.

Brady saw the compassion that softened Anna's expression and realized that while she might say no to him, she could never refuse a child who needed her help.

"I'll want to run my own tests," she said, not looking at him. "It'll help me plan my therapy. Jennifer and I can do those now. You can pick her up in a few hours."

"I'll be back around two."

Brady kissed his niece good-bye. "Don't be afraid," he whispered. "Everything's going to be fine."

Anna watched the exchange with interest. Brady Matthews obviously loved his niece very much. For Jennifer's sake, Anna would have to put aside her personal feelings for the man. Jennifer needed her help. That was all Anna needed to know. In the end, it was all that mattered.

Three hours later, Anna put down her pencil and smiled. "You're doing great,

Jennifer. One more test and we'll be through."

Jennifer looked longingly at the plate of chocolate chip cookies. "Just one more?"

"Your uncle will skin me alive if he finds out how many cookies you've had. You don't want him to get mad at me, do you?"

Jennifer shook her head. "No. But do we have to tell him?"

Sharing conspiratorial smiles, they each took another cookie. The test completed, Anna gave Jennifer a puzzle to work while she compiled her findings for Brady Matthews.

Ten minutes later, she sat opposite him on the sofa, her legs crossed beneath her.

"Your niece has dyslexia — a type of learning disability — and a focusing problem. Though dyslexia isn't curable, it can be treated. It's the kind of disability that can go undetected for years, especially with a bright child like Jennifer."

"What about the focusing problem?"

"That can be corrected with eye exercises and glasses."

He grimaced. "She's not going to like that."

For the first time since Brady had met her, Anna smiled.

Caught off guard, he blinked. The smile transformed her face from merely pretty to beautiful, bathing it in light.

"Most kids don't," she said, drawing his attention back to the matter at hand. "But she'll get used to them."

As he listened to her outline for the treatment she'd planned, he studied the woman before him, impressed by her thoroughness and confidence. "When can we start?"

"School's out in another week. We could start after that."

"Sounds good. About fees —"

She shook her head. "That's not important."

"It is to me. How much do you charge?"

She named a ridiculously low figure. He countered with a more reasonable amount.

Anna looked as if she might protest.

"I believe in getting the best and paying for it." He looked around. "Or don't you need the money?"

She bristled. "Yes, I need the money. But I don't need it so much that I'd turn away a child who needs my help."

"Fine. Then you won't mind accepting a decent wage."

"No," she said doubtfully.

"Then it's settled." He squared one leg over the other. "How did you get along with Jennifer?"

41

All traces of doubt vanished from her face and she smiled warmly. "Fine. She's a delightful little girl. You must love her very much."

"I do. We'll see you next week." He hesitated. "Try not to worry too much about your brother. These things have a way of working themselves out."

"I hope so."

He took her hand, liking the feel of it. It was small but strong. Like her. There were no rings, he noted with interest. "Thanks for taking us on."

Anna stared after him, confused by the conflicting feelings she was experiencing. Brady Matthews, the uncle, was far more disturbing than Brady Matthews, the cop. She'd felt his concern for his niece and knew it was sincere.

It was that sincerity that convinced her to agree to tutor Jennifer, even though common sense dictated that she stay as far away from him as possible. She wondered why he had insisted she be Jennifer's teacher. He had both put her at ease and disturbed her at the same time.

Anna frowned, puzzled over her reaction to a man she barely knew. He wasn't handsome; his face had too many angles and planes for that. And yet, those same angles and planes made him appealing.

His brown hair, cut military-short, emphasized a deep tan. But his eyes — so dark as to be almost black — had snagged her attention. They looked as though they'd seen man at his worst and still managed to believe in his basic goodness.

She shook her head, annoyed by her reflections. Brady Matthews was the uncle of one of her students. Nothing more. Deliberately, she turned her thoughts to Jennifer.

There was nothing complicated here, but she studied the test results once more. She'd known what she was going to find, but she had to make sure. Jennifer was definitely dyslexic. Reading, to a dyslexic, was like trying to fit a puzzle together with one of the pieces missing. Anna intended to supply that missing piece.

For the first time in two days she felt a lifting of the cloud that had hovered over her life. This was something she understood. Helping a child learn to read was the most wonderful thing in the world. Nothing else even came close to the thrill she experienced every time she helped a child find that missing piece of the puzzle. Jennifer would be reading before the summer was over, Anna promised herself.

A smile erased the lines of strain around her mouth as she picked up a pad and pencil and started roughing out the first week's lessons for Jennifer.

The smile dimmed as she thought about Jeff. If only his problems were so easily solved.

CHAPTER THREE

Brady studied the report in front of him. Jeff Lancaster had a history of juvenile offenses. Minor stuff, but a conviction for possession of drugs could land him in juvenile hall this time. Brady's thoughts returned to Anna Lancaster. She didn't deserve this kind of trouble.

He frowned as he remembered her reluctance to accept any money for tutoring Jennifer. The lady was obviously dedicated to her work. He guessed she could use the extra money, but he'd almost had to force her to accept a reasonable salary. Once again he was impressed by her.

He'd vowed to be home on time tonight, having promised Chad and Jennifer a trip to a local pizza parlor. They'd had too few treats in their lives lately.

"Hey, Matthews, you going to stare at your desk all day?" Jim Davies demanded. "I've got a couple of tickets to the game tonight. You want to go?"

Brady looked up. "Sorry. I'm taking Jennifer and Chad out for pizza."

Davies grinned. "Never would have figured you for the domestic scene."

"Neither would I," Brady agreed, chuckling.

A year ago, Brady would have jumped at the chance to go to a game. But a year ago he'd been on his own. Any free time he had now was spent with Chad and Jennifer. The surprising thing was that he liked it. His only regret was that he had to be away from home so much.

A smile tugged at his mouth as he thought back over the last year. In a short time, Chad and Jennifer had managed to turn his life upside down and inside out . . . and he wouldn't have had it any other way. Looking back, he admitted he'd been frightened at the idea of being solely responsible for them.

His sister's death had been a shock, though he had known it was coming. She'd suffered from cancer for a year before she'd succumbed.

"Great pizza, Uncle Brady," Chad said an hour later through a mouthful of pepperoni, sausage, and cheese. Tomato sauce outlined his mouth clown-fashion.

"Yeah, great," Jennifer seconded as

cheese dripped from her lips.

Brady barely suppressed a grin at the two pizza-covered faces across the booth from him. "Glad you like it."

"Can we come here every night?" Chad asked.

"Don't be a dope," Jennifer vetoed. "Then it wouldn't be special anymore."

"Your sister's right," Brady said before Chad could retaliate.

"How 'bout every other night?" Chad persisted.

"How 'bout you finish your salad?" Brady countered.

Two hours, three ice cream cones, and a trip to the video arcade later, Brady decided he was too old for all this. Chasing down felons was less hair-raising than keeping up with these two. It was also infinitely less satisfying, he thought, as Chad hugged him tightly before climbing into bed.

"Thanks, Uncle Brady. It was the best night ever."

Brady ran a hand through Chad's hair. "We'll do it again."

"Soon?" Chad murmured, his eyes drifting closed. Long lashes fanned across his cheeks, creating half-moon shadows.

"Real soon," Brady promised. He bent to kiss the boy's cheek. " 'Night, slugger," he whispered, and tiptoed from the room.

Brady knocked at Jennifer's door. He'd already learned that little girls wanted and needed more privacy than did little boys.

"Come in," she called.

He smiled as he found her brushing her hair in front of the small dressing table he'd built for her. Watching her, he thought how much she looked like his sister. A lump lodged in his throat.

"You're going to be as pretty as your mother," he said, crossing the room to stand behind her.

"Do you really think so?"

"I know so."

"Mom used to brush her hair each night," Jennifer said. "A hundred strokes."

"I remember." He waited until she'd laid the brush down. "C'mon, sweetheart. It's bedtime for you."

Brady skimmed a kiss across her forehead as he tucked her in. " 'Night, pumpkin."

" 'Night, Uncle Brady."

He was about to close the door when she said, "Uncle Brady?"

"Umm?"

"I love you."

The words wrapped themselves around his heart, weaving a spell of their own, and a pleasant warmth settled over him. "I love you, too."

"I know."

Her easy acceptance gratified him. Chad was young enough to settle quickly into a new routine — one that didn't include his mother — but the jury was still out as far as Jennifer was concerned.

Brady had the impression that she was waiting for something. Waiting for him to screw up? He'd given her plenty of reasons in the past to think that he might. Now her words gave him hope that she would begin to regard him as a permanent part of her life.

He watched her for a moment before closing the door, an incredible feeling of love welling up inside him.

Tossing his jacket aside, he stretched out on the sofa. Not for the first time, he was worried. Taking care of two children made police work look easy. His sister would have been faster to catch on to Jennifer's problem. But Leigh was dead, and it was up to him to see that Jennifer got the help she needed.

His thoughts returned to Anna Lancaster. He had a feeling about her, one that told him she was going to be important in his life.

She was Jennifer's tutor, of course, but he sensed more than that. Right now, he didn't want to examine that too deeply. Right now, he wanted only to remember her soft voice — a voice which made him think of warm honey — and the way it made him feel.

Anna drew a small circle in the center of the chalkboard. "Press your nose against it."

Jennifer did as directed. "What's this supposed to do?" she asked, her voice muffled.

"You'll see. Now stay right where you are, but draw ten circles clockwise around this one. Try to make them as much like the one I've drawn as possible."

Jennifer giggled as she drew the circles.

"Now look at what you've drawn," Anna said.

Jennifer stepped back and looked at the board. Her lip trembled. "Mine look all wobbly, like a baby drew them."

They both trained their gazes on the series of circles, each of them a different size and shape. Some were closed, while others resembled lopsided C's and S's.

"That's right. That's our problem." Anna smiled, slipping an arm around Jennifer's shoulders. "After a couple of lessons, you're going to be drawing beautiful circles."

They repeated the exercise ten more times. By the end of the lesson, both of them were laughing.

A knock on the door alerted Anna to the fact that they had company. She found Brady at the door, his squad car parked outside.

"Care to see what we're doing?" she invited.

He followed her to the workroom.

"Uncle Brady, look at this!"

Brady Matthews looked at the series of misshaped circles scrawled on the board and then scowled at Anna. "I thought you were supposed to be teaching her to read. Instead I find you playing games."

She motioned him into the kitchen, calling over her shoulder, "Keep practicing, Jennifer. I'll be back in a minute."

In the kitchen she turned to face him. "Detective Matthews, these exercises are teaching Jennifer to focus. Do you have a problem with that?"

"No . . . but you'll have to admit it looks pretty silly."

"Only to an adult. Once she accepted that drawing circles is okay, she started having the time of her life. Listen to her."

High-pitched giggling could be heard

from the back room.

"Maybe," he conceded. "But I still don't see what this has to do with reading."

"Everything. Jennifer can't start reading until she learns to use her eyes properly. The first step was the glasses you got her. Now she's learning how to see again. It's also excellent for her balance and focusing problem."

He looked unconvinced. "If you say so."

She heard the doubt in his voice but couldn't blame him. The exercises did appear foolish to many adults.

"Learning to read is like learning to walk. You have to start with little steps before you can take big ones. That's what Jennifer's doing right now — taking little steps."

"I hope so. Look, I apologize. I didn't mean to doubt your ability, it's just that —"

"You're worried about her. I'd be concerned if you weren't. But she needs your support a lot more than your worry. Children take their cues from the adults around them. If you think this is silly, she'll start thinking that too."

He threw up his hands in mock surrender. "You've convinced me."

"Good. Now go in there and tell her you're proud of her. She needs that more than anything."

He did just that. Anna watched him, impressed with the about-face he'd made.

After giving them a few minutes together, she said, "Same time Thursday, Jennifer?"

"You bet!" Jennifer scampered off to the car, leaving Brady and Anna alone.

"I'll see you Thursday," he said, and let himself out.

Anna put away her equipment and rubbed her back. Many people thought teaching was a desk job, one that required no physical exertion. *Boy, were they ever wrong.* She chuckled at the idea of teaching students to read from behind a desk.

She grabbed a glass of juice and a handful of crackers before her next student arrived. This was her favorite part of the job — actually working with children. The paperwork involved was necessary, but she would never muster as much enthusiasm for it.

Anna spent the late afternoon evaluating test results. Each child needed a different approach; it was up to her to see that she chose the right one.

A door opened and closed. Footsteps pounded up the stairway.

"Jeff, is that you?"

A slammed door was the only response.

Anna climbed the stairs and knocked at Jeff's door. "Can I come in?"

"I'm busy," came the muffled reply.

"It'll just take a minute." She heard shuffling, then the slam of a drawer.

"All right, already. I'm coming." He opened the door, his expression resentful and somewhat scared.

"What were you doing in here?" she asked.

"Putting away a few things. You're always on my case about cleaning up, so that's what I'm doing."

She looked over his shoulder but he blocked her view of the room. Pasting a bright smile on her face, Anna said, "Great. But I'm not such a slave driver that I'd make you miss dinner. It'll be ready in fifteen minutes."

"Uh . . . thanks, but I'm not hungry. Maybe later."

"You know the rules. You eat when it's served, or you don't eat."

"Big deal. What are we having? Meatloaf again?"

"No. I fixed hamburgers and fries."

"Oh." Jeff reddened when she named his favorite meal. "I'll be down in a few minutes."

Anna searched his face, trying to understand what went on there. He seemed angry at her, though for what she had no idea. But it didn't take much to set off his temper these days. She curbed a tired sigh that hovered at her lips.

The door inched shut.

She took the hint. "I'll give you a call when it's ready."

"Great," he said, closing the door.

Anna stared at the blank wood, feeling that Jeff had closed more than a door in her face. Why couldn't he see that she only wanted to help him? Every time she tried to talk about the case, he clammed up, almost as though he didn't trust her. But that was ridiculous. She was his sister. Surely he knew she would never hurt him.

He was trying, she thought fifteen minutes later as she watched him put down two burgers and a plateful of fries. He laughed and smiled but his laughter was forced, his smile strained.

That was the problem. They had to work to get along with each other and it was becoming more of a struggle every day. The easy relationship they'd shared in the past was just that — in the past.

They said an awkward good-night. Anna went to her workroom, intending to plan her lessons for the next day. For once, though, her mind wasn't on her work. She was listening for some sound from Jeff's room. It was too quiet, too still.

Hating herself for her suspicion she climbed the stairs and knocked lightly at Jeff's door. When there was no answer she pushed it open and found what she had dreaded.

An open window was mute evidence of his departure. The empty room offered no answers as she sank down on the bed. This time the tears would not be stemmed.

She was determined to have it out with Jeff the next day but he disappeared before she'd crawled from her bed. She felt stiff and cramped from spending half the night on the sofa, waiting for him to return.

A knock at the door interrupted her thoughts. She answered it, grateful for the opportunity to think about something else.

Brady stood on her front porch, his face set in harsh lines.

"Our lesson isn't scheduled until eleven," Anna said, puzzled. "Is something wrong with Jennifer?"

"No," he said curtly. "She's fine. Jennifer told me you said all reading is off-limits."

She sighed, knowing what was coming. Folding her arms across her chest, she prepared for battle. "That's right."

"Why?"

"Because she needs —"

"Why isn't she reading *something?* Even *Dick and Jane* would be better than nothing. Seems to me you'd have her reading more things, not telling her to stay away from books altogether. Look, Ms. Lancaster, I know you mean well, but I'm not so sure you're the right teacher for Jennifer after all. All she talks about is how much fun she has here, the toys you let her play with."

She drew a deep breath. "I can understand how you might feel that way, but I do know what I'm doing. Detective Matthews —"

"Brady," he corrected.

The phone rang. Hoping it was Jeff, Anna hurried to answer it.

"It's for you," she said, unable to hide her disappointment.

Brady picked up the receiver. "Hello? Yeah. I'll be there right away." He replaced the receiver. "That was the precinct. I've got to go."

"Of course." She hesitated. "If I can convince you that learning to read *is* play, will you let Jennifer come back?"

"That's a big if. What if you don't convince me?"

"I'm willing to take that chance," she said with more confidence than she felt.

"Tomorrow?" he suggested. "I'll tell Jennifer something came up and you had to cancel. Then I can take her lesson. Okay with you?"

She nodded. Watching him leave, she wondered if she'd made a mistake. Convincing Brady that her methods worked wouldn't be easy. He'd be a difficult observer, not content to simply sit and watch.

That gave her an idea. He *wouldn't* just sit and watch. She'd put him through the same routine she used with Jennifer. Anna smiled. By the time they were finished, Brady was going to believe she knew what she was doing.

Her smile tapered off. She was a good teacher. She'd be able to convince Brady to let her continue teaching his niece. What worried her more was spending time alone with him.

Without Jennifer there to act as a buffer between them, they might very well come to blows. No, Anna admitted, that wasn't the truth. The truth was much simpler.

She was afraid to spend time alone with Brady because she was starting to like him altogether too much.

CHAPTER FOUR

Brady was as punctual as it was possible to be. Anna had expected nothing less. Nevertheless, she was flustered when she opened the door.

It hadn't been a good morning.

Another run-in with Jeff had left a bad taste in her mouth. To top things off the air conditioner, which had been limping along the last few days, finally died. Her budget wouldn't stretch to cover a new one so Anna opened all the windows, set fans at strategic spots, and prayed the temperature wouldn't reach the 90's.

She led Brady into the kitchen and offered him a cup of coffee.

He accepted it with quiet thanks, took a sip, and then set it aside. "Listen, Anna, I know you care about your students. That's why I wanted you to tutor Jennifer. But it's going to take some fancy explaining to convince me that she should be playing games instead of reading."

Anna took a deep breath, knowing the next minutes were crucial. "It's important that Jennifer not read anything until she learns to reuse her eyes. Until then, she's just hurting herself. She may become so frustrated that she won't even want to try anymore."

She pushed a strand of hair back from her face and hoped she didn't look as hot and frustrated as she felt.

"She's always reading," Brady said. "That's what I don't understand. She reads every evening to me."

Anna shook her head. "What you've heard is Jennifer repeating what she's memorized. It's a common trick. Children memorize a passage, sometimes even pages. I've seen adults do the same thing."

"Why?"

"Because confessing that they can't read is too humiliating. People will go to any length to cover it up."

"And all along, that's what Jennifer's been doing — covering up?"

"I'm afraid so." Anna hesitated, unsure how to ask the next question. "What about Jennifer's mother? Was she aware of anything?"

"Leigh was so sick the last year of her life, I doubt she knew what was going on.

60

If she'd been well, she'd have picked up on it."

"I'm sure she would have."

"But why didn't I see it? I knew something was bothering Jennifer, but I figured it was the adjustments she'd had to make in the last year."

"Don't blame yourself. Like I said, kids can be pretty clever when it comes to covering up, especially a smart kid like Jennifer. She's so adept at it that she probably doesn't even realize she's doing it anymore. It's automatic."

"Then how do we break it?"

"First, no reading. Not yet. When she's ready she'll read. Until then she's not to even look at the back of a cereal box."

He grinned. "You too, huh?"

"I was one of those kids who read everything in sight. Including the backs of cereal boxes."

"Me too," he said. "I used to read all about the athletes and pretend I was one of them."

"I'd pour the cereal out of the box so I could do the puzzles."

"You must have driven your mother crazy."

She smiled, remembering. "I probably did. She never complained, though. She always made me feel like I was terribly clever for figuring them out."

"She sounds like a special lady."

A shadow crossed Anna's face. "She was. She died last year."

Brady touched her arm. "I'm sorry."

"Thanks." His simple, sincere words touched her, and she fought back the tears that still came too easily. She hadn't allowed herself to think about her mother lately. Even after a year, it still hurt too much.

"Looks like we've both lost someone we cared about," he said.

"Somehow it doesn't get any easier, no matter how old you are."

"And you're so old," he teased.

"Twenty-six."

"That old, huh? Makes me feel ancient. I'm thirty-two."

"That *is* old," she agreed, a hint of amusement belying her serious tone.

"The kids make me feel every year of it. And then some."

"They can do that. I love my work, but sometimes I feel like the walking wounded by the end of the day. Kids have more energy than I ever dreamed of having."

Brady checked his watch. "Mind if we get started with the lesson? I've got to be at the precinct in two hours."

"Fine. This is my favorite place in the house," she confided as she led Brady into her workroom.

She followed his gaze around the room as he took in the balance beam, the swinging chair suspended from a chain, the miniature trampoline. Brightly colored open cubes formed a tunnel that could twist and turn according to a child's whim.

"It looks like a child's fantasy," he said.

She smiled, pleased with his reaction.

"Do you use all this with every child?"

"No. The swinging chair and the cubes are for the more severely learning-disabled children. They provide stimulation. Also, many of these children have a very short attention span. We may go from one activity to another within a couple of minutes. The more activities I can provide, the better."

He nodded.

"You're still not convinced, are you? You think Jennifer should be sitting at a desk with her nose pressed in a book."

"No . . . But this looks like more like a gym than a classroom."

"I hope so." She saw his frown and knew she had her work cut out for her.

Anna put him through the routine she'd worked out for his niece. "I'm going to hold out one of my hands. I want you to slap it as fast as you can. You have to watch both hands at the same time."

"You're kidding, right?"

She didn't answer but held up her open hand.

Brady slapped it, watched, slapped again. After five minutes he wiped his brow, now beaded with sweat. "What good does this do?"

"None for you. But it trains Jennifer to use both eyes together. Now I'm going to spread my hands further apart."

They continued the exercise until Brady held up a hand in protest.

"Enough already." He wiped a hand across his brow.

After he had walked on the balance beam, swung in the chair, and crawled through the cubes, she asked, "How do you feel?"

"Exhausted." He panted heavily, as though to prove his point. He lay down on the mat, hands laced behind his head. "Mind if I ask you a question?"

"You can ask."

"How did you finance all this? Equipment like this doesn't come cheap."

Anna looked uncomfortable. "I didn't

64

rob a bank or anything, if that's what you mean."

He frowned. "You know that's not what I meant. I was just wondering how you managed to put together a setup like this on a schoolteacher's salary."

"I bought it a little at a time. Right now, I want to get a new monitor. But . . ."

"What's the problem?"

"Money," she said flatly. "There's never enough."

"That's for sure." He looked at her curiously. "What about a government grant? A program like yours would certainly qualify."

"It might."

"What's the catch?"

"In order to qualify, I'd have to comply with state regulations. That means cutting back on things I think are important, having larger classes, you name it." She grimaced. "I wasn't willing to take orders from people who wanted to turn my school into a reading mill and me into a drill sergeant."

Brady found his respect for her growing. "Did you always want to be a teacher?"

She nodded.

"No dreams of being the first woman astronaut, or President of the United States, or CEO of General Motors?"

"I guess I'm a throwback. From the time I was five years old I knew I was going to be a teacher. A reading teacher."

"Why a reading teacher?"

"Why not?"

Brady sensed there was more to it than what she'd told him, but decided not to press her. He intended to get to know Anna better. There'd be time enough for questions later.

"Are you always this nosy?" she asked. The smile hovering at her lips removed any sting from the words.

"Only about people who interest me."

"And I interest you?"

"You interest me very much."

He noted the blush that smudged her cheeks and smiled to himself. Anna Lancaster was a fascinating paradox of 1990's independence and old-fashioned modesty. He found he liked the combination. Liked it a lot.

"How's your brother?" he asked. He'd been to the house several times and hadn't seen Jeff yet.

"All right," she said. "He's job-hunting right now."

"Any luck?"

He watched as a shadow crossed her

face, wondering at the cause of it. "Not yet. Not many people want to hire a seventeen-year-old boy."

Especially a boy who's in and out of trouble, he added silently. Surprising himself, he said, "Maybe I can help. I have a friend at a lumberyard who's looking for summer help."

She looked at him gratefully. "That'd be great if you could. Jeff's a hard worker, and he's strong. I know he'd do a good job."

He wondered if she was even aware of the doubt that robbed her voice of conviction. She was more troubled about her brother than she let on.

"Let me see what I can find out."

"Th . . . thank you." The stammer in her voice was echoed by the hitch in his breath as he looked at her. Her eyes, wide and appealing, told him how much this meant to her.

"What about Jennifer?" she asked, reminding him of his purpose in being there. "Are you going to let her continue with the lessons?"

"I think I have to. After the workout you put me through I know you're the right teacher for her." He held out a hand. "Friends?"

She placed her hand in his. "Friends."

"I've enjoyed our conversation," he said, surprised to find it was true.

"So have I."

"Maybe we can do it another time."

"I'd like that."

Brady picked up the pamphlets she'd given him. "I'd better be pushing off. Thanks again."

"Don't mention it."

At the station his thoughts centered on Anna Lancaster. Annoyed that the woman had had such an effect on him, he concentrated on remembering that she was Jennifer's teacher, nothing more. In fact, given the situation with her brother, he'd do well to stay away from her.

But the stern warning didn't help keep his thoughts in line. They tended to dwell with increasing frequency on her — the way her eyes lit up when she talked of her work, the softness of her voice, the scent of her hair.

Silently, he admitted what he'd already known: Anna Lancaster was quickly becoming important to him. Just how important he wasn't sure. The corners of his mouth lifted in a half smile. He was looking forward to finding out.

"Hi, Sis." Jeff tossed his jacket on a chair

and then picked her up and swung her around. When he set her down, he kissed her cheek.

"What's all this about?" she asked, laughing.

"The new me. I decided I'd better start shaping up. You know, get a job like you've been nagging me to, pick up my junk. Otherwise, you might decide to kick me out."

"No chance of that. But I have to admit, I like the idea of a little help around here. And getting a job would be great."

"Yeah, well, don't expect too much," he warned. "Most places want a high school grad."

She started to say he could get his diploma if he only went back to school but stopped herself in time. They'd been over that ground too many times for her to suggest it again. When — if — Jeff went back to school, it would have to be his decision.

She reached up to hug him. "Welcome back, Jeff."

"Yeah."

He eased out of her arms, reminding her that hugs weren't welcome anymore. She swallowed her disappointment and focused on what he was saying.

"Anything to eat?"

She laughed. "Some things never change.

But tonight we're celebrating the new you. We're eating out."

"No kidding?"

"No kidding," she said, apologizing silently to her checkbook, whose balance was already precariously low.

She let Jeff choose the restaurant and tried not to grimace when he drove to the local burger hangout, where the noise level was exceeded only by the amount of grease deemed necessary to saturate the food.

"Don't you ever get tired of those?" she asked as he downed his third Burger Deluxe.

"Never," he mumbled between mouthfuls. "Don't you want yours?"

Anna looked from her Special Burger covered with secret sauce to her ketchup-smothered fries. "I'm full."

"Mind if I have it?" he asked, transferring it to his plate before she could answer.

"Would it matter?" she asked good-naturedly.

"No."

They both laughed.

He polished it off in two bites.

It felt good to laugh together. It had been too long since she and Jeff had actually had fun with each other. Anna knew she bore a good deal of the blame. She'd spent too much time nagging him — about school, work, his friends — and too little time simply being with him.

She couldn't change the past, but maybe she could start making the present and the future better.

She paid for their meal and was about to leave when she spotted Brady and Jennifer on the other side of the room. Before she could change her mind, she walked over to say hello.

"Brady," she said.

He stood, a pleased smile on his face. "Anna. It's good to see you. You know Jennifer. And this is Chad," he said, pointing to a blond boy.

"Hi, Miss Lancaster," Jennifer said shyly.

Anna motioned to Jeff to join them, but he hung back. "I see you're having the Deluxes," she said to Brady.

He grinned. "Is there anything else?"

"Not for my brother, anyway." She glanced back at Jeff. "He's waiting. I guess I'd better go."

"See you tomorrow," Brady called after her.

"Why didn't you join us?" she asked Jeff as they drove home.

He didn't answer. A speculative gleam entered his eyes. "Who are they?"

"Brady Matthews and his niece and nephew. I'm tutoring Jennifer. I told you about her, remember?"

"Yeah, I remember. He's the cop, right?"

"Something wrong with that?"

Jeff gave her an odd smile. "No. Nothing wrong at all. You know, Sis, I think everything's going to work out just fine."

"So do I."

As she slid into bed that night, she remembered Jeff's odd words. A quiver skittered down her spine. She didn't try to understand it; somehow, she knew she didn't want to know the answer. Not now. Not when everything seemed to be going so well.

She glanced at her calendar, the date circled in red marker an unwelcome reminder that she and Jeff had a court appearance in two days. If only the judge would give Jeff a suspended sentence. She dared not let herself think of what would happen if he didn't.

Jeff wasn't bad. He'd just gotten mixed up with the wrong people. Somehow, though, that particular argument was wearing thin.

The next morning, she rose, still excited over Jeff's "new start." This was the moment she'd been waiting for. She'd give him every bit of support he needed, she promised herself.

Once more, she thought back over the past year with more than a trace of regret. Since their mother's death, she and Jeff had grown apart, each handling their grief in their own way. She'd been so absorbed in trying to come to grips with it that she might have neglected her brother.

Though it hadn't seemed so at the time, she latched on to that now as the reason for Jeff's changed behavior. She pushed away the nagging doubt that there was more wrong with Jeff than that simple explanation suggested. Somehow, it seemed disloyal. If he wanted to turn his life around, she was more than willing to help.

With that in mind, she told him of Brady's offer as they fixed breakfast together. He grabbed her arms, startling her so that she spilled the orange juice she was pouring.

"What gives you the right to interfere in my life?"

Anna tried to hide her shock at his reaction by blotting up the juice. "I was only trying to help, Jeff. Brady was nice enough to set up this interview. The least you can do is show up."

"What if I don't want to work in some

crummy lumberyard? What does it pay, anyway? Minimum wage?"

"So what if it does? You'd be lucky to get it."

"Working for peanuts? You gotta be kidding."

"What kind of job do you want?"

"Something that pays enough to make it worth my while."

"You sound like you ought to be earning twenty dollars an hour."

He hooked his thumbs in his jeans and rocked back on his heels. "Why shouldn't I?"

"Because you're just a kid who hasn't even graduated from high school yet. The kind of job you're talking about takes a diploma. Maybe even college."

"Not if you know where to look. Tell your cop friend thanks, but no thanks. I'll get my own job." He slammed down the plates and grabbed an apple.

"What about breakfast?"

He gave her an insolent look. "Sorry. Something spoiled my appetite."

"Jeff, wait!" she called, but he'd already taken off.

She looked at the elaborate breakfast they'd cooked together and sighed, her own appetite now nonexistent.

"Nice going," she muttered to herself. She'd managed to push him further away, just when things were looking up.

She waited dinner, hoping, praying Jeff would show up. When he did, he headed straight to his room, muttering something about not being hungry.

The scene was repeated the next morning. He was careful to speak to her only when he had to. They moved about the house as polite strangers, careful not to be in the same room for more than a minute.

The strain had flayed her nerves until she wanted to shout at him, demand to know why he'd turned into a stranger. But, of course, she couldn't. She was the adult, the responsible one.

CHAPTER FIVE

"Come on, Jeff, we're going to be late."

"I'm coming."

The surliness in his voice inched its way through the calm she was trying to hold on to. Anna bit her lip. Anything she said now would only make things worse. She knew he was scared. *She* was scared too.

The trip to the courthouse was made in silence. She glanced at Jeff, wanting to reassure him that everything would be all right. But the words caught in her throat, perhaps because she wasn't at all sure they were true.

He stared straight ahead, the ever-present scowl on his face more pronounced than usual. She reached out to squeeze his hand but he moved it out of her reach.

She tried to ignore the stab of pain she felt at the snub. He probably thought she was trying to baby him. And maybe she was, she acknowledged. He'd told her so often enough. But the habits of a lifetime were hard to break.

Inside the courthouse, she looked around before taking a seat.

A hand on her shoulder caused her to start. "Sorry," Brady said. "I didn't mean to scare you."

"You didn't. I'm just a little jumpy." She looked at his dark business suit. "Are you here officially?"

"Unofficially. I thought you might need a friendly face." He slipped into the seat beside her and squeezed her shoulder.

The warm pressure of his hand was almost her undoing. She blinked rapidly to control the tears that were dangerously close. "Thanks."

"Don't mention it."

They turned their attention forward as Jeff's case number was read.

"How does the defendant plead?" the judge asked.

Jeff and his public defender rose. "Guilty, Your Honor."

"Does the state wish to make a statement?"

The assistant district attorney rose and gave a summary of the charges against Jeff.

Jeff's lawyer rose. "Your Honor."

"Go ahead," the judge said.

"The defendant is a juvenile, Your Honor, not a hardened criminal. I hope the court will take his age into consideration when passing sentence."

The assistant D.A. stood and droned on about troubled juveniles being a danger to society. Brady only half-listened, his attention riveted on the woman sitting beside him.

He placed his hand over hers, surprising himself with the gesture. With her eyes too big for her face she looked vulnerable and scared. He'd have done the same for anyone.

Maybe not for anyone, he admitted with innate honesty. There was something special about Anna, something that drew him to her.

He'd known what an ordeal this would be for her; he couldn't let her face it alone.

He shifted his gaze to Jeff. The boy's defiant attitude had evaporated during the hearing. Brady only hoped it would vanish completely. For the first time Jeff looked like what he was — a scared seventeen-year-old boy.

When the judge pronounced a suspended sentence of six months and forty hours of community service, Brady heard Anna's sigh of relief. He looked at her small hand, now resting inside his own. He doubted she even knew he held it.

He was glad Jeff had been given a suspended sentence but he couldn't help wondering if some time in juvenile hall would have done Jeff more good than community service. Ordinarily, Brady was all for service hours in place of incarceration, but in Jeff's case he wasn't sure. The boy had a chip on his shoulder. Brady just hoped it got knocked off before it grew to the size of a boulder.

"Hey, it's all over," he whispered to Anna.

She turned to him, her eyes dark with unshed tears. "I was so afraid he'd have to go to juvenile hall."

"I know, honey. But he didn't." He didn't add that another offense would probably land Jeff there.

He gently freed his hand. Crescent shaped grooves scored his palms where her nails had dug into his flesh. "Good thing this didn't go on any longer," he teased. "My hand couldn't take it."

She followed his gaze. "Oh, Brady, I didn't know . . . Why didn't you say something?"

His joke, intended to distract her, had backfired. "And miss the chance of holding hands with the prettiest girl in the court-room? No way."

She smiled as he'd hoped she would. "Thanks for being here. I don't think I'd have made it without you."

Though he knew she spoke without thinking, her words sent a rush of warmth through him. "You'd have done fine." As he said the words, he knew they were true.

Despite her fragile looks, Anna Lancaster was a survivor. Whatever the circumstances, she'd done what needed to be done. He couldn't help comparing her to her brother and reflecting that it was too bad Jeff didn't have the same kind of guts.

Jeff smiled cockily and swaggered toward them. "See, Sis, I told you. Piece of cake."

"You were lucky," Brady said. "Six months in juvenile hall is no picnic."

Jeff snapped his fingers. "I could do that standing on my head with one arm tied behind my back."

"Jeff, what's gotten into you?" Anna asked. "You had a narrow escape. I hope you realize that."

"Oh, I do, Sis. I do. Right now, I gotta tell the guys. Catch you later."

He sauntered off without waiting for a reply.

Brady watched as Anna twisted the strap of her purse around her arm.

"He didn't mean that the way it sounded. He's just relieved that it's over," she said. "I'm sure he's learned his lesson."

"Sure." Brady wondered whom she was trying harder to convince — herself or him. "Why don't I take you to lunch? I'll bet you didn't eat any breakfast."

She gave a sheepish grin. "You'd be right. I was too nervous."

"Come on. I know a place that does great Buffalo wings." He slipped an arm around her shoulders and guided her out of the courtroom.

Twenty minutes later they munched companionably on barbecued chicken wings and baked beans. Brady watched as Anna licked her lips in enjoyment. She'd lost the pinched look she'd worn during the trial.

"How 'bout some more?" he asked, gesturing to the platter.

"No, thanks. I've already eaten more than I should. But you were right — they're great. Do you come here often?"

"Every chance I get." He wanted to keep her talking, keep her from thinking about Jeff. "Have you always lived here?"

"Since I was nine years old. We moved

here after my father . . . after he left. How about you?"

"Born and raised in Salt Lake."

"Ever thought of moving?"

"No way. I'm a Utah boy through and through. I love this city, even with all its problems." He checked his watch. "I hate to cut this short, but I'm on duty in another hour."

"Thanks for lunch . . . and for being there."

"You're welcome." He brushed her cheek with his lips. "If I get a chance, I'll call later."

"I'd like that."

After dropping her off at her car, he drove to the station. His morning's absence would cost him extra time tonight but it had been worth it. He knew her too well to think she'd ever ask for help, but she'd needed a friend today.

He was glad he could be there for her.

He remembered Jeff's parting words and wondered what the boy was up to now. Obviously, his brush with the law hadn't affected him as much as it had his sister. Brady could only hope that the next time Jeff was hauled in, it wouldn't be for something more serious. That there would be a next time, he had no doubt.

But for Anna's sake, he hoped he was wrong.

After her morning's absence from work, Anna put in extra hours at her desk, trying to work up another budget proposal. The figures hadn't changed from the last time, though, and she sighed. The problem was always the same. There was never enough money for the "extra" programs.

The shortsighted attitude was going to cost more in the long run. Scrimping pennies only to spend dollars later on. She pushed her hair back from her face and looked at the clock. Four o'clock and she hadn't accomplished a thing.

Ten more minutes, she promised herself, and she'd call it quits. But ten minutes stretched into twenty, then another twenty. A glance at her watch an hour later sent her scrambling for her purse and paper. She planned to fix a special dinner of all Jeff's favorites tonight.

With the trial behind them, maybe they could make a fresh start. Right now, she desperately needed to believe that everything was going to be all right.

She stacked the papers in the desk drawer and regretfully said good-bye to the long, hot bath she'd been fantasizing about since noon.

She was just frosting the cake when Jeff arrived home. "In here," she called. "We're having a celebration dinner."

"Hey, great," Jeff said, swiping his finger through the bowl of icing.

Dinner passed pleasantly and Anna allowed herself to believe it really was a new beginning for her and Jeff. Not until they started to clean up did her hopes crumble.

"I liked your lawyer," she said.

"He's a jerk."

She put down the dirty dishes and turned to face him. "Jeff, he convinced the judge to let you off with probation and community service. How can you call him a jerk?"

"Okay, okay, he's all right. Satisfied?" Jeff shoved dishes into the dishwasher and slammed the door. "The important thing is, he got me off. Of course it didn't hurt having you and your boyfriend sitting there in the front row holding hands. Judges like that kind of thing, especially when the boyfriend's a cop."

"Brady's not my boyfriend." Anna felt the heat rising in her cheeks. "He's only a friend. He came because he was concerned about you."

"Not about me, Sis. About you." He

laughed, a harsh, cynical croak that had nothing to do with amusement. "I have to hand it to you. That was a pretty smart trick, going out with him. I wasn't sure at first." He gave her an admiring look. "I didn't know you had it in you."

She looked at him in bewilderment. "I don't know what you're talking about. I tutor Brady's niece. That's all."

"Sure, sure," he soothed. "Look, I've got to go out. Catch you later."

"Jeff, wait. I thought we might catch a movie or something."

"Later," he called over his shoulder.

Anna started after him and then stopped. What could she say to him?

His comments about her and Brady troubled her. Jeff hadn't actually accused her of using Brady, but he'd hinted at it. The thought left her feeling dirty. She knew it wasn't true, but what if Brady thought the same thing?

She stewed over it the rest of the night. Over dinner the following evening, she tackled Jeff about it.

"I don't like what you implied about Brady and me. I don't use people. Not for you. Not for anyone."

He gave her a knowing grin. "Sure you don't."

"Brady is the uncle of one of my students. And a friend. That's all."

"Yeah, sure. I get you."

"I don't think you do."

Jeff cocked a hip against the counter. "Why did you agree to be the kid's tutor if you didn't plan on cozying up to him?"

"Jennifer needed my help."

"Mike said you'd deny it, but let me tell you, he was pretty impressed. Not many guys have a sister with a cop for a boyfriend, especially a cop who's willing to put in a good word for them."

"Where did you hear that?"

"Mike's got a couple of friends who pick up things. Word is, Matthews stuck his neck out, recommended I get a suspended sentence."

She didn't believe it. Brady had too much integrity to use his job to get Jeff off lightly.

"You're wrong."

"Hey, Sis. Take it as a compliment. The pig must like you a lot." He gave her an assessing look. "I wonder why."

She stared at him, seeing him — really seeing him — for the first time. For once she didn't sugarcoat what her eyes told her was true. She didn't like what she saw. "If you think I'd ask Brady to compromise his job for you, you don't know me. Or him."

She started to brush by Jeff but he grabbed her arm. "I don't know what your problem is, just don't go messing things up for me. All right?"

She shrugged off his hand. "I don't know you anymore, Jeff."

"I didn't mean anything by it," he said, looking suddenly subdued. "I was just kidding."

"Were you?" Without giving him a chance to answer, she walked away.

In her workroom, Anna sank down on a chair. She picked up the grant proposal she was preparing for the school board and started editing it.

An hour later, Jeff opened the door and smiled at her as if nothing had happened. He bent over to kiss her cheek. "Thought I'd say good-night."

She was through playing his games. "Good-night." She went back to her editing, but Jeff didn't leave. Instead, he perched on the corner of her bed.

"Was there something else?"

"Sis, I need some money."

"What for?"

"A guy's got expenses. You know."

"No, I don't know. Why don't you tell me?"

"Look, Anna, I just need a few dollars

till I get a job. No big deal."

She paused. Jeff never called her by her name except when he was in trouble. "What's wrong?"

"Nothing. I'm broke and need some bread."

"Jeff, don't lie to me. Something's wrong."

He shifted his gaze away from her. "I owe a guy some money."

"How much?"

"Couple hundred."

"Two hundred dollars?"

He nodded. "I . . . uh . . . borrowed it from a friend and now I have to pay up."

"A friend?"

He pressed his toe into the carpet. "Mike."

"Mike's no friend."

"He's the only friend I've got." A wheedling note entered his voice. "I need the money, Sis. Are you going to come through or not?"

"I can't, Jeff. We're already behind with the bills. And the bail money . . ."

"Sure, chalk that up to me. I didn't ask you to bail me out."

"Jeff, talk with Brady. He'd help. I know he would."

"Don't be a dope."

She touched his arm. "Let me tell him, Jeff."

He looked undecided. For a minute she thought he was going to agree.

"I'll work it out myself. No sweat."

Sleep didn't come easily, her dreams haunted by Jeff calling for her, begging for her help. But she couldn't reach him. When she did, it was too late.

She slept through her alarm and woke only fifteen minutes before her tutoring session with Jennifer was to start.

When Brady dropped his niece off he took one look at Anna's face and demanded, "What's wrong?"

She started to brush it off but he wouldn't let it drop. "Don't tell me 'nothing,' because I won't believe it," he said. "Something's wrong, and I'm not leaving until you tell me what it is."

Reluctantly, she repeated last night's conversation to him. "Who could he owe that kind of money to?" she wondered aloud.

Brady frowned. He could think of several possibilities, none of them reassuring. "He didn't say anything else? Why he borrowed the money in the first place? Anything?"

She shook her head. "Only that he owed Mike two hundred dollars."

"Do you think he'll talk to me?"

She bit her lip. "I don't know."

"Want me to give it a try?"

"Please."

That evening, as he sat across from Anna's brother, Brady wondered what he'd taken on. Jeff looked through him with the arrogance of someone who knew all the answers before any of the questions were asked.

He slouched in front of the television. His glassy-eyed stare struck a nerve and Brady glanced at Anna to see if she understood the possible significance of it.

She turned off the set. "Jeff, Brady wants to talk with you."

"Do you mind? I was watching something."

"A rerun of 'Gilligan's Island'?"

Stepping around her, Jeff turned the TV back on. "I happen to like it."

"Anna, maybe you could make us some coffee or something," Brady suggested.

She glanced uncertainly from him to her brother before nodding.

Ignoring Jeff's scowl, Brady turned off the TV and lowered himself to the lumpy couch, squaring one leg over the other. "I hear you've got a problem."

"Nothing I can't handle."

"Care to talk about it?"

Jeff shifted his gaze away from Brady. "It's no sweat. I'll work it out."

"I know you're in trouble. Why don't you tell Anna before she finds out for herself?" Brady's eyes narrowed as he watched Jeff glance nervously toward the kitchen.

"Just because you're dating my sister doesn't mean you've got the right to mess with my life. Why don't you go arrest some little old lady for jaywalking? Isn't that what you cops do best?"

Brady held his temper. "If you won't talk to me, there are counselors —"

"I don't need a shrink. I'm fine. Now lay off." The boy jumped up, paced around the room, and then slumped back in the chair. He fidgeted with the fringe on his western style shirt, his fingers never still. "Why don't you save it? You don't care about me. You're here because of my sister."

"I'm here because Anna's worried about you. I am too."

"What's it to you?"

"I'd like to try to help you," Brady said quietly. "If you'll let me."

"I don't need your help. Yours or anyone else's."

"Then you're not as smart as I thought you were."

"I'm plenty smart, mister. Smart enough to know that all you care about is scoring points with my big sister."

"That's where you're wrong. I do care about you. I care about anyone in the kind of trouble you're in."

A tremor of fear crossed Jeff's face. "You're crazy."

"I know you're involved in something you can't get out of." Brady was only guessing, but from the look on Jeff's face his guess had been all too accurate. "Why don't you tell me? Maybe I can help."

"No one can help," the boy muttered. "Why don't you get out of here? Tell big sis you've done your good deed for the day and leave me alone."

"If you won't tell me, there are other people who can help you."

"I don't need your help. I don't need anyone's help!"

"Jeff, think about Anna. She doesn't need this kind of trouble. She deserves better."

For a moment he thought he'd gotten through to the boy as Jeff appeared to digest what Brady had said.

But Jeff only shrugged.

Anna walked into the room. "I found some cookies. I thought you might like —"

Jeff stood suddenly, thumbs hooked in

his jeans. "Tell your boyfriend to mind his own business."

Brady took the tray from her and set it on the coffee table.

She glanced from him to Jeff. "What's wrong?"

Brady waited, hoping Jeff would tell her, but the boy refused to meet Brady's gaze and stalked from the room.

Brady took a deep breath. He'd blown it. Big time. Now he had to face Anna and tell her he'd alienated Jeff even further.

"What did you say to him?" she demanded.

"I tried to get him to tell me what's bothering him, but he refused."

"Look, Brady, I know I asked you to talk with Jeff. I know you're trying to help, but maybe it'd be better if you didn't —"

"Stick my nose in?"

She gave a sheepish smile. "Something like that."

"You're right. It's none of my business."

"I didn't mean it like that. It's just that Jeff's been my responsibility for a long time now and —"

"You don't want anyone else telling you how to take care of him. I'm beginning to understand that since Jennifer and Chad came to live with me."

"It's not that I don't appreciate what you're trying to do. But I know my brother. He's been in trouble, but nothing serious."

Brady had his own ideas about what was wrong with Jeff. He prayed he was wrong, but the boy's insolent attitude, the personality changes Anna had described, the friends he hung out with, added up to one thing.

"Have you ever wondered if Jeff might be using drugs?"

The horrified look she gave him caused him to sigh inwardly. No one wanted to admit their child . . . or their brother . . . might be taking drugs.

"Of course not. Jeff's not the type. Sure, he's been in some trouble, but drugs? No. Up until last year he's been on the football and basketball teams. He has too much respect for his body to use drugs.

"Brady, I'm grateful for what you're trying to do, but you're way off base about Jeff. He's a good kid. I know him. He'd never do anything like that."

He knew when it was time to back off. Maybe he was wrong. It wouldn't be the first time.

"I'm sorry. I guess I've been a cop for too long."

"It's all right."

The coolness in her voice belied her words. It wasn't all right. Far from it.

Good going, Matthews. You've managed to alienate both the brother and the sister in one night.

"I'll call you tomorrow," he said.

"Fine."

He tried one more time. "Talk to him, Anna. Find out what's bothering him."

"Jeff's my problem. I'll take care of him."

He knew he'd hurt her, but what was he supposed to do? Every instinct told him that Jeff was into something a lot more serious than Anna realized. If she weren't so close to him, she'd see it too.

Brady saw she was close to tears. He wouldn't help matters by staying. "I'm sorry. I'd better go. I'll call you tomorrow."

Outside, he slammed his fist into his hand. He'd managed to antagonize Jeff and offend Anna at the same time. The department had strict rules against getting involved with someone he met through work. He was beginning to understand why.

CHAPTER SIX

"We were at a birthday party and everyone was supposed to read a nursery rhyme out loud and then act it out. When it was my turn, I started to read. I knew the words. But I couldn't say them."

Anna heard the pain and humiliation in Jennifer's voice. She ached for the little girl and wished she had an easy answer. Unfortunately, there were no easy answers.

Just as there were no easy answers for Jeff, she reflected. After Brady had left last night, she'd spoken with Jeff again. She'd still been worried about the money he claimed to owe Mike Rafferty. But Jeff had brushed off her worries, telling her Mike had given him some more time.

"Chad reads better than I do," Jennifer said, drawing Anna's attention back to the present. "Even the first graders at school read better. I'm *never* going to learn." Her voice cracked and she looked away.

"You *are* going to learn to read," Anna promised. "But it won't happen overnight. Remember, we talked about taking it one step at a time."

"I didn't think it would take so long," Jennifer wailed. "I'm still doing those stupid exercises while my friends are playing or going to the mall."

"I thought you liked the exercises."

"I do. I *did*," Jennifer corrected herself. "But they're for babies. And I'm not a baby."

"I know you're not. And I know you're upset."

But Jennifer wasn't listening. "Next year I'm supposed to start middle school. If I'm held back . . ."

Anna resisted the urge to tell Jennifer that that wasn't going to happen, knowing her young friend needed honesty, not sympathy. Also, she sensed there was more going on here than the possibility of being held back a year. "Are you upset about being held back or about what your friends might think?"

When Jennifer didn't answer, Anna asked, "What did your friends say?"

"They said it was no big deal."

Anna gave a silent prayer of thanks that

Jennifer's friends hadn't teased her about not being able to read. Children could be cruel at times, but they could also be extraordinarily sensitive.

"I'll bet you can do things that no one else can. Each of us has different talents. The trick is to find them."

"A lot of them can't do long division, like I can," Jennifer said thoughtfully.

"See? And pretty soon you'll be reading rings around them. But you've got to keep doing the exercises."

"Even if they're stupid?" Jennifer grumbled.

Anna bit back a smile. "Even if they're stupid."

They spent the next hour on the balance beam. Jennifer wore a look of determination that Anna was coming to recognize. She'd seen the same expression on Brady's face.

"Good job," she applauded when Jennifer finished a series of exercises, first forward, then backward, carefully placing one foot behind the other.

"Thanks. Snacktime now?"

"You sound like my brother."

"How old's your brother?"

"Seventeen. He's out job-hunting right now." She mentally crossed her fingers, hoping she was right.

As Jennifer chewed on a cookie, she said, "Do you like Uncle Brady?"

Anna almost choked on her cookie. "Of course I like him."

"I mean *like* him. Girlfriend-boyfriend liking."

"Your uncle and I are friends. That's all."

"Are you sure?" Jennifer looked unsatisfied. "He likes you. I can tell."

Distinctly uncomfortable now, Anna stared at her glass of milk. "Jennifer, your uncle and I are friends. That's all."

"You're sure?"

Anna made an imaginary cross in the air over her heart. "I'm sure."

Jennifer looked relieved.

"Anybody here?"

Grateful for the interruption, Anna jumped up. "We're in here."

Brady walked into the therapy room.

He looked tired, she thought. "You work too hard," she said without thinking, and immediately blushed at her runaway tongue. She had no right to say that. He was nothing more than the uncle of one of her students.

But Brady didn't seem bothered by her observation. "You're right. Tell the bad guys to let up and maybe we could all take a breather." He pulled Jennifer into his arms. "How'd the lesson go today?"

Jennifer didn't answer but only looked at Anna.

Anna exchanged a glance with Brady. "Jennifer, why don't you get your uncle a cookie and some milk?"

She slipped from her uncle's arms. "Be back in a minute."

When she left the room, he turned to Anna. "Did something happen?"

"She was upset about the party."

Brady looked surprised. "She told you about that?"

"We spent most of the hour talking about it. I think she's feeling better now."

"Thanks. I tried to talk to her about it, but nothing I said was right."

Jennifer returned then, munching a cookie, preventing Anna from saying anything more.

"Hey, where's mine?" Brady asked.

Jennifer clamped a hand to her mouth. "Oops. I forgot."

All three of them laughed.

"It's all right," Brady said. "Jennifer, why don't you wait in the car? I'll be out in a minute."

Jennifer gave them an uncertain look before leaving.

"Are you still worried about the party?" Anna asked. "I think Jennifer's feeling all right about it now."

"No, I'm not worried about Jennifer or the party." He paused. "I wanted to apologize about last night. I was out of line."

"I'm the one who should apologize. I asked you to talk with Jeff and when you tried to help, I threw it back in your face."

"How about we both agree to accept each other's apologies?"

"I'd like that," she said softly.

"I like you, Anna."

"Oh . . . Well, I like you too."

"That's not what I meant. But it'll do for now." He leaned closer to skim his lips along her neck.

"Brady, be serious."

"I am serious." His lips traced the line of her jaw before he lowered his head. "I've wanted to do this for a long time now." He kept the kiss brief because he knew she wasn't ready for anything more.

He saw the questions in her eyes, questions he shared because he was as confused by what was happening between them as she was. But he had no answers. Not yet. Soon, he hoped. But not yet.

"I'll be seeing you."

Anna stared after him, bemused by the

kiss. As kisses went, it had been as insubstantial as butterfly wings. She put a finger to her lips. The contact had been so brief, she might have imagined it except for the warmth she felt there. Yet it had shaken her more than she liked to admit.

She'd been kissed before. But none of those kisses had affected her as much as had Brady's gentle caress. Maybe it wasn't the kiss but the man who'd reached her when others had failed. The thought made her shy away from further analysis.

She'd been right, she decided. Brady Matthews, the man, was a force to be reckoned with. If she wanted to keep her heart intact she needed to remember he was the uncle of one of her students. Some of the day's brightness dimmed as she acknowledged what she already knew. A future between them was impossible. And not only because of Jennifer.

Her eyes clouded with pain as she accepted the other reason she couldn't dream of a future with Brady: Jeff. She and Jeff were a package deal. No man wanted to take on a teenage boy, much less one with problems. Her ex-fiance had made that clear enough a year ago.

When the call came, Brady had a feeling

in his gut about it. He'd learned not to ignore those feelings. More than once they'd saved his life.

But this one was different. This wasn't the pricking of hairs at the back of his neck warning him of danger. It was one of dread, dread of what they'd find.

The apartment building stank of rotting garbage, backed-up sewage, and decay. But overriding everything was the stench of despair. It was in the air, in the faces of the children who peered from doorways, in the eyes of the woman who pressed herself against a wall.

Brady spotted a pay phone at the end of the hallway. Had she made the call?

When he and Jim found the girl, she was already so strung out she couldn't even give them her name. Brady saw the needle first. Only a few inches long, it shouldn't have looked like a lethal weapon.

She weaved, then staggered before she fell. Brady caught her only a moment before she hit the ground.

"I can't get a pulse," Jim yelled.

Together, they began the drill. "Breathe," Brady prayed, hardly aware he spoke aloud. "Breathe."

"I've got a pulse," Jim shouted.

At the same moment, Brady heard the soft whoosh of air. It wasn't much, just a thread of sound he'd have missed if he hadn't been so attuned to every sense.

When the ambulance arrived, Brady and Jim stood back, relieved to let the paramedics take over. Brady took one last look at the girl's pale face. Somebody's daughter, somebody's sister, she belonged to *someone, somewhere*.

Was there someone worrying about her, wondering where she was, if she was all right? A search of the apartment gave no clue to her identity.

They followed the ambulance to the hospital. There was nothing they could do, but by tacit consent, they wouldn't leave until they knew.

"She's going to make it," the doctor said, coming out of the ER forty-five minutes later. "Giving her CPR when you did made the difference."

"Thanks, doctor."

Brady experienced the exhilaration of relief, but it was short-lived. Back at the station he tried to concentrate on work but found his mind wandering to the girl he and Davies had left in the hospital.

She'd been so young, scarcely older than Jennifer. It was that that burned inside him. Some animal was selling drugs to children.

Brady clenched his fist, wanting to ram it into a wall. The bitterness in his mouth had a name.

Rage.

He felt it, tasted it, and knew it was poison. A cop couldn't afford to become emotionally involved. How many times had the order been hammered into him? How many times had he said it to himself?

It was easy enough to believe it when he sat in a squad room listening to a lecture on the importance of remaining objective. It was almost impossible to put it into practice when the victim had a face, when the victim reminded him far too much of his niece.

He looked at the report he was filling out and tried to remember why he'd wanted to be a policeman.

Right now, he didn't know.

That he and Jim had gotten to the girl in time was small comfort compared to the fact that yet another child had overdosed and almost died on the drugs that were steadily invading the city.

He felt like the small boy who'd tried to plug the dam by sticking his finger into the hole. Only in this case there were thousands of holes. Each time one was plugged, ten more sprang up.

He wanted . . . no, needed . . . to talk through his feelings with someone. Jim Davies was a good friend, but Brady knew Jim was struggling with his own feelings. He'd scarcely spoken on the ride from the hospital to the station. He didn't need Brady dumping on him. The department shrink? No way.

The answer was so simple he wondered why he hadn't thought of it before.

Anna.

He needed to see Anna.

When his shift was over, Brady headed to her house. Outside her door, he hesitated. Would she even see him after last night? What would he say to her? That he was going crazy and needed to talk with someone who'd understand? He'd almost talked himself out of it when the door opened.

"Hi," he said, feeling all kinds of a fool. "How did you know I was here?"

"I saw you walking up the sidewalk. I kept waiting for the bell to ring, but it never did."

He shuffled from one foot to the other. "I was trying to decide how much of a fool I wanted to make of myself. But first I wanted to apologize about last night. You were right. I had no business telling you how to handle Jeff."

"You were just trying to help."

"So you're still talking to me?"

She smiled. "Of course. Come on inside." She waited until they were settled on the sofa before asking, "Is something wrong with Jennifer?"

"No. Jennifer's fine. I . . ."

"Brady, what's wrong?"

"Nothing's wrong. I don't even know why I'm here tonight. I wanted to talk with someone. And . . ."

"I'm glad you came."

"Am I interrupting something?"

"Yes."

He turned to leave, but she motioned him to sit down. "I was balancing my checkbook. Believe me when I say you arrived just in time."

"Problems?"

"Nothing that a couple of hundred dollars won't fix." She smiled. "But that's not what you came to talk about."

"No," he said. "It's not."

"Tell me, Brady."

He looked at her eyes, filled with patience and compassion. If anyone could understand, this woman could.

"We found a girl today. Not much older than Jennifer. Strung out so bad we didn't think she was going to make it."

"Did she?"

"Yes."

"But something's still bothering you." She folded her hands around his. "I want to understand. Help me."

He took his time. Slowly at first, he told her about the young girl, the words spilling out faster as he relived the panic of trying to revive her.

"She's going to live. But for how long? How long until she tries it again?"

"You saved her, Brady. That's what matters. You can't worry about the future. There's enough pain in the present." Her next question surprised him. "Why did you become a cop?"

At one time, the answer would have been easy. At one time, he'd known all the answers. Or thought he had.

But now he wasn't so sure. He'd grown up. He was no longer the young, idealistic cop who'd been so sure he could right all the world's wrongs.

He groped for the words, trying to help himself, as well as her, understand. What had once been so clear was now muddied with the experience only harsh reality can bring. "I wanted to make a difference. To help people who couldn't help themselves.

When I came home at the end of the day, I wanted to know that somehow, something I'd done mattered." He gave her a rueful smile. "Pretty corny, huh?"

"It's not corny at all. And you are making a difference. Every day, you put yourself on the line to help others."

"I'm not so sure anymore." He paused, trying to make sense of it in his own mind before he put it into words.

"If you'd rather not . . ."

"No. It's not that."

"What is it then?"

"I don't know if you'd understand." He laughed quickly. "I don't even know if I understand anymore."

"I'm listening," she said, the quiet sympathy in her voice breaking down his usual reluctance to talk about his job.

"It used to be so simple. There were the good guys and the bad guys. The good guys wore white hats, the bad guys wore black ones."

"Like the Lone Ranger and the bank robbers."

He smile. "Yeah. I grew up on reruns of the Lone Ranger. Then it was Kojak and all the rest. The good guys always won in the end."

"And now?"

"Now we're lucky if we break even. Half the creeps we haul in are back on the street before we've even finished with the paperwork. The others . . ."

"What about the others?"

"The others are victims themselves. One night I found someone breaking into a grocery store. Turned out to be a mother trying to get food for her kids. Seems they hadn't eaten in over two days. She'd run away from a husband who beat her. Said she stuck it out with him until he started beating on the kids. Then she knew she had to get out. She'd probably never even had a parking ticket before, and she's forced to steal to feed her kids."

"What did you do?"

"I took her and the kids to get something to eat at a fast-food place. Then I gave her bus fare to get to Colorado where her parents lived. I don't even know if I did the right thing. I broke every rule in the book."

Anna slid her fingers down his cheek. "You're a good man, Brady. You *do* make a difference. Because you care."

"I don't know if it's enough anymore."

"It's enough."

The quiet conviction in her voice had him looking up, wanting to believe and yet not daring to. "How do you know?"

"Because it has to be. If all of us who cared suddenly stopped caring, the world would be in a bigger mess than it already is."

He hadn't thought of it that way before.

She cupped his face in her palms, forcing him to look at her. "If you stopped being a cop, what would you be?"

"I don't know. Ever since I can remember, I wanted to be a cop. I never wanted to be anything else."

"You're a good cop. What you do makes a difference. Don't ever think it doesn't."

Her words touched something inside him, something he'd thought long buried. He felt like that young policeman once more, fresh out of the academy, wanting to change the world, and believing he could. He looked at her in wonder. Anna had given him back that most precious of all gifts — hope.

"You're quite a lady," he said quietly.

"I'm talking to quite a cop."

He laughed softly. "Sounds like some kind of mutual admiration society."

"Yeah. We'd better quit before we get really sloppy."

But he didn't want to quit. He wanted to spend time with her, not as an uncle with his niece's teacher, but as a man with a woman.

"Anna, I know this is sudden, but would you have dinner with me? Tomorrow? Just the two of us? I want time alone with you. Time without interruptions."

She smiled a smile that made him think of warm summer nights and soft music.

"I'd like that."

Brady waded through the sea of paperwork that overflowed from his desk. The afternoon had dragged by, punctuated by the kinds of interruptions he normally took in stride. Now, though, they'd niggled away at his patience and temper.

"If we spent a fraction of the time tracking down bad guys as we do filling out forms, we might be winning out there," he said, motioning to the window and the streets below.

Jim Davies grinned. "Admit it, Matthews. You like this stuff." He picked up a form in triplicate and flipped through it. "Pink, yellow, white. What more could a man ask for? Except maybe a cute little schoolteacher with blond hair and big blue eyes."

Brady and Jim had been partners too long for Brady to take offense. He wasn't particularly surprised to find that Jim knew of his growing interest in Anna. He hadn't tried to keep it a secret. "How about a partner who knows when to keep his mouth shut?"

Jim held up a hand. "Sure thing." His voice lost its bantering tone. "She seems like a nice lady. Classy. But her brother . . ."

"Yeah," Brady sighed. He'd already gone through the ethics of dating someone whose brother was under possible investigation. But the key word was possible. Aside from one bust and a couple of pranks, the department didn't have anything on Jeff. Not yet, anyway.

Jim pushed himself up from the desk where he'd slouched. "If you want to talk about it, let me know."

"Thanks, Jim."

Brady waited until his friend had left before punching out the hospital number. A fingerprint check had turned up a name and home address for the girl he and Jim had found yesterday. Her parents had been contacted and had rushed to the hospital.

His job was over, Brady told himself. Still, he hung on while the operator put him on hold before connecting him with the floor nurse. He wanted to know for himself what was happening with the girl.

A few minutes later, he replaced the receiver, smiling. She was being released in a week and going home with her parents. Maybe, just maybe, everything was going to be all right for once.

Preparing to leave, he pushed work from his mind and concentrated on the evening ahead, surprised to find he was nervous. He grinned. A simple dinner date had him as sweaty-palmed as a schoolboy. Even so, he was looking forward to it more than he had anything in a long time.

A glance at his reflection in the window wiped the smile off his face. His hair needed a trim and his shirt and jacket had definitely seen better days.

He checked his watch. If he hurried, he'd have enough time. After a quick trip to the mall and the barber shop, he was smiling.

"Wow, Uncle Brady, you look great," Jennifer said when he returned home wearing one of the new shirts and jackets he'd bought.

He swung her high into the air. "Thanks, pumpkin."

"Are you going out?"

"I asked Anna to have dinner with me."

"Like in a date?"

He grinned. "That's right. What do you think? Will she like the new me?"

"You promised you'd help me with my exercises tonight."

"We didn't set up any special time, did we? We'll do it tomorrow night, okay?"

"I guess so," Jennifer said in a small voice. She disappeared into her bedroom.

Brady frowned. *Something was bothering her.* He had started to follow her when Chad bounded into the room.

"Hey, Uncle Brady, look at this." Chad shoved a paper bag under Brady's nose.

Cautiously, Brady opened it. A dead rat. Not a mouse, but a rat. "Uh . . . that's some rat, Chad. Wh . . ." He cleared his throat and tried again. "Where'd you get it?"

"I traded my calculator to Tommy Baker for it. Pretty cool, huh?"

A calculator for a dead rat? He exhaled a long breath, remembering what he'd paid for the calculator. "Yeah. It's pretty cool, all right."

"You aren't going to make me trade back, are you?"

Brady weighed the possibilities. A calculator or a small boy's self-esteem? "No, Chad, I'm not going to make you trade back. Only you'd better not show it to Mrs. Barney. She might not understand about rats."

"Okay." Chad sniffed inside the bag. "It smells."

Brady tried to control the twitching of his lips. That was an understatement. "Why don't you put it outside? Tomorrow I'll help you bury it."

"That'd be great. I'll bet no one else has a dead rat buried in their yard."

He'd learned a long time ago not to bet on a sure thing. "You're probably right."

"Can we make a tombstone and everything for it?"

What the heck? What was a dead rat buried in the backyard with a tombstone marking the spot compared to Chad's obvious excitement? "Sure."

Chad threw his arms around Brady. "Thanks, Uncle Brady. I knew you'd understand."

"You're welcome. Chad?" Brady took in the dirt-stained face, the grubby hands clutching the bag, and knew an overwhelming sense of love.

"Yeah?"

"I love you."

"Me too."

"Chad? One more thing."

His nephew looked up.

"Be sure to wash your hands before dinner."

Chad trotted off to the bathroom, leaving Brady chuckling behind him.

It was nice, he decided an hour later sitting across the table from Anna, just looking at her. She'd worn her hair loose tonight. Her lips were pink, and she smelled of wildflowers. She'd also kept him at a distance with a steady stream of impersonal subjects. He intended to put an end to that right now.

"Do you think we've made enough small talk?" he asked.

"Is that what we've been doing?"

"We've talked about the weather, Jennifer's reading, and Chad's dead rat. I'd say that qualifies as small talk."

Her lips curved into a smile. "I'll plead guilty to the first two, but Chad's dead rat is definitely not small talk."

Brady felt an answering smile at his lips. She hadn't been repelled by the story of the rat. Instead, she'd laughed until tears ran down her cheeks.

"You handled it just right," she said.

"Did I? Afterward, I wondered if I should have told Chad to get his calculator back."

She shook her head. "That wouldn't have made anyone feel good except you. And Chad would've been humiliated."

"Yeah, that's what I figured."

She laughed again.

Brady liked her laugh. It was soft and low. It rippled over him in gentle waves.

"You should do that more often," he said, taking her hand and stroking the soft skin on the underside of her wrist.

"What?"

"Laugh. You don't do it enough."

She seemed surprised. "I don't?"

"Not nearly enough." He continued holding her hand, liking the feel of it in his. "I wonder why."

Her smile faltered, and she withdrew her hand from his.

"Hey, I didn't mean anything."

"It's okay. It's just that it's been a hard year."

The waiter arrived then with their meals. Hungry after skipping lunch, Brady started in on his prime rib. He'd taken several bites before he realized that Anna was only pretending to eat.

Gently, he took her fork from her and laid it on her plate. "What's wrong?"

"Nothing."

"Nothing doesn't make you frown like that."

"I was thinking of Jeff."

"You're worried about him."

She nodded. "I don't know how to help

him. We used to be so close. Now everything I say is wrong."

"You have to let him grow up sometime. He's not a kid. Whatever decision he makes is because he wants to."

"You make it sound so simple. But he's only seventeen. I can't just turn my back on him."

"I didn't suggest you do that, only that you let him start taking responsibility for what he does."

She lifted her head. "You sound like you've been through this before."

"Not personally. But I've seen too many parents willing to assume blame for the trouble their kids get into, when it's the kids who need to take the responsibility."

"I'm not trying to be his mother."

"No?"

"No." But her voice lacked conviction. "It's not easy letting go," she finally said.

"No, it's not. But you can't keep blaming yourself for Jeff's screwups."

She took a sip of wine. "I'd rather not talk about it anymore, if you don't mind." Her voice was decidedly cool.

"I'm sorry, Anna. I didn't mean to lecture you."

She managed a wobbly smile. "I know."

He decided a change of subject was in

order. "Let's talk about something else."

"What did you have in mind?"

"You."

"Me?"

"Don't look so surprised. You make a great topic."

Faint color tinted her cheeks. "What makes you think so?"

"A reading teacher who spends her own money teaching other people's children to read, who refuses to take a salary when it's offered, who takes time to convince a stubborn cop that she knows what she's talking about."

"Stop." She held up a hand in protest. "You make me sound like some kind of saint."

"Uh-uh. Just someone who cares." His voice softened. "Someone I'd like to get to know better."

"I'd like that too," she said quietly. "What do you want to know?"

"You said you'd always wanted to be a teacher."

"That's right."

"Why a reading teacher?"

She looked out the window. He followed her gaze, but he sensed she was seeing something far different than the mountains that reached up to meet the sky.

"My mother couldn't read. She had dyslexia, like Jennifer. But no one recognized it back then. The teachers just thought she was dumb.

"She got the typical labels — slow learner, unmotivated, discipline problem. Pretty soon she just quit trying. She dropped out of school when she turned sixteen."

"So that's why you decided to become a reading teacher."

"You make it sound so idealistic. I didn't feel that way about it. I just wanted to help kids who, for whatever reason, couldn't read. Mom encouraged me. She worked two jobs to help put me through college.

"She was a waitress at a local diner. She'd bring the menus home. I'd help her memorize them. When the owners changed the menus, she'd have to memorize a whole new list. She had to change jobs pretty often. It was rough for her."

Silently, Brady filled in the blanks, knowing she was leaving out much more than she said. "It must have been rough for you too. I don't guess you had much of a social life."

"Don't get me wrong," Anna said. "We managed all right. But I knew she was always embarrassed at not being able to read. She couldn't even read enough to pay the bills."

"What did she do before you were old enough to help?"

"She always managed to have a friend over when it was time to pay the bills. Then she'd conveniently misplace her glasses or pretend she had a headache and couldn't concentrate." Anna smiled sadly. "It's like I told you. People, including adults, develop all kinds of tricks to compensate. They're too embarrassed to admit they can't read."

"That's a high price to pay for pride."

"Think about it, Brady. Who wants to admit she can't read when most of us take it for granted?"

Her tone, more than her words, caused him to pause. She was right. Even at nine years old, Jennifer was ashamed that she couldn't read, too ashamed to tell him. How much more devastating it must be for an adult to admit to the same problem.

"When did you learn your mother couldn't read?"

"When I was five. I saw her trying to read the directions on the back of a box of cake mix. All of a sudden, she started crying. I asked her what was wrong.

"After that, I started reading for her.

Recipes, street signs, the mail. I was reading before I started school."

"You had to grow up fast."

"It wasn't bad. Mom was great. Even though she had to work, she was always there when I came home from school. She made the world's best molasses cookies. Later on, when Jeff came, she stayed home for a year to take care of him."

"Where was your father?" Brady asked gently.

"He had a gambling problem. I barely remember him. Mom said that one night he went out to get a gallon of milk and never came home."

She said it so matter-of-factly that he knew his sympathy wouldn't be welcome.

"How old were you?"

"Nine. Jeff was still a baby. He doesn't even remember our father. But we never felt deprived. Mom saw to that."

"She sounds like a special lady."

"She was. Even though it's been a year, I still miss her."

"There's no timetable on getting over the loss of someone you love," he said.

"No, there's not. You must have loved your sister very much."

He nodded, unsure how to describe his relationship with his sister. She'd been sick for so long. Near the end, he hadn't even been able to kiss her because of all the tubes. It'd been hard on Jennifer and Chad. He coughed to cover the lump in his throat.

"She was sick for a long time. I tried to do what I could . . . for her and for the children."

"I'm sorry."

He took her hand in his. "Thanks. It helps, talking to someone about it. Most people tiptoe around it, afraid they'll say the wrong thing."

"I know. When Mom died I wanted to talk about her, remember all the good times. But . . ." She shrugged. "People don't like to talk about death. It makes them uncomfortable."

He nodded, remembering back to the first awful weeks after Leigh had died. Friends avoided the subject as though bringing it up would intensify the pain. Though he had appreciated their well-meant efforts, he had wanted to talk about Leigh, share memories of her with those who'd known her well.

"Jennifer seems remarkably well adjusted," Anna said. "From the little I saw of Chad, I'd say he was too."

"They're good kids. I just wish I didn't

have to be away so much. Mrs. Barney stays with them when I'm working, but it's not the same."

"No, it's not. But don't sell yourself short — you're doing a great job with them."

"Thanks. I think I went through every book the library had about raising children when Jennifer and Chad arrived at my house." He laughed ruefully. "But nothing could have prepared me for the real thing. Being a single parent is a lot rougher than the books make out."

"You can say that again."

He heard the wistfulness in her voice and knew she was still worried about Jeff.

"We've gotten awfully serious," Anna said.

"Yeah. I didn't mean to dump all this on you."

"It's all right. I'm glad you told me."

"So am I."

He didn't have to ask himself if she was telling the truth. It was there in her eyes. The burden he carried seemed lighter after sharing it with her.

She didn't play the games so many of the women he'd dated did. She said what she meant, nothing less, nothing more. He liked that. He liked everything about her.

Brady checked his watch. He didn't want

the evening to end, but he'd pulled the early shift tomorrow. Regretfully, he signalled for the check.

The night wrapped itself around them as they drove home. Brady didn't feel the need to talk; simply being with Anna was enough. Apparently, she felt the same, for she, too, was silent.

"I'd like to do this again," he said after he walked her to her door.

"I'd like that too."

The gentle smile at her lips made him think of the kiss he'd placed there a day ago.

He suited action to thought and lowered his head to brush his lips over hers, barely skimming them. "Good night, sweet Anna." After sliding his palm down her cheek, he left.

Brady shifted the car into gear and headed home, his thoughts centered on Anna.

Anna was a special woman. She'd shown it with her concern for Jennifer. She'd shown it with her concern for Jeff. She'd shown it with her quiet understanding as she'd listened to him tonight.

Sweat beaded on his lip as he realized what he wanted. He wanted more than an evening with Anna.

He wanted a lifetime.

CHAPTER SEVEN

The day had gone from bad to worse. His IN basket overflowed with "priority" matters, while the OUT basket remained empty. Brady looked at the growing stack of paperwork that littered his desk and wondered if it was possible that reports reproduced themselves overnight.

The fanciful notion had him doubting his sanity. He pressed his fingers to his temples and tried to concentrate on something pleasant. He didn't have to search far.

Anna.

Just thinking of her eased the tension that gnawed at his neck and shoulders. He didn't stop to think about it. He picked up the phone and punched out her number.

"Jennifer and Chad have been begging me to take them on a picnic in the mountains," he said without preliminaries. "I need reinforcements."

"So that's what I am? Reinforcements?"

He could hear the smile in her voice and

felt one of his own twitching at his lips. "Let's just say you'd make the day a lot more fun. For me."

"What does a reinforcement have to do?"

"Well, mainly she has to field the questions when I run out of answers. Those two can ask more questions than a team of defense lawyers at a murder trial."

"Kids are good at that. Have they asked you why the sky isn't blue all the time?"

"Not yet, but I expect it's coming any day now. That's why I need you along. A teacher knows those things."

"Not this teacher. I'm still trying to think up a good answer to that one."

"If you'll come, I promise you won't have to answer more than ten questions. Fifteen, tops."

Her laugh, low and sweet, drifted over him. "How can I refuse such a generous offer?"

Brady grinned. "You can't."

"You're right. I can't. What can I bring?"

He wasn't sure she'd come. Only now did he admit to himself how much he wanted to see her, to be with her, to listen to her laugh. After Thursday night, he'd been afraid she'd refuse. Not that he'd have blamed her. Breaking up a fight between

128

him and her brother couldn't have been pleasant.

"I asked what I should bring," she reminded him.

Just yourself was his first response, but he thought better of it. "How are you at making chocolate cake?"

"Are we talking the bakery type with fancy flowers or the gooey kind with gobs of icing that dribbles down the sides and gets all over your hands and face when you eat it?"

He smiled, thinking of Jennifer and Chad. "The gooey kind, definitely. The gooier the better."

"Then I'm great."

His smile grew broader. "A woman after my own heart. I'll pick you up at ten. Wear comfortable shoes. We'll be hiking up the canyon."

"Does this expedition call for boots, or will sneakers do?"

"Sneakers will do just fine."

Brady found himself smiling for the rest of the day. In less than five minutes, Anna had succeeded in wiping away the frustrations of the day. She'd done it by simply being herself.

That she could have such a strong effect on him didn't annoy him any longer. More and more, he was realizing how much she'd come to mean to him. He'd started thinking about happily-ever-afters with Anna.

When he told the kids that Anna was joining their picnic, Chad whooped delightedly. Jennifer didn't offer any comment. Now that Brady thought about it, Jennifer hadn't mentioned Anna once in the last few days. Usually she was full of stories of what they'd done during her lessons. It was "Anna this" and "Anna that." Now, though, Jennifer was strangely quiet about her teacher.

"How's your reading coming, pumpkin?" he asked that night as he tucked her in.

"Okay, I guess."

"Just okay?"

"Yeah."

"What're you reading now?"

"*Treasure Island.*" She chewed on a fingernail, a habit he thought she'd broken. "It's not the real thing. Anna calls it a simplified version. But it's pretty neat."

"That was one of my favorites. I'll bet Anna makes it —"

She squirmed out of his arms. "Can't we talk about something else?"

He looked at her in surprise. "Is something bothering you?" Confronted by silence, he tried again. "Has something

130

happened between you and Anna?"

"No . . . But that's all you talk about. Anna this and Anna that. I don't want to talk about her anymore."

Brady studied her small earnest face, so like his sister's. "I thought you liked Anna."

"I do. I'm just tired of hearing about her, okay?"

Though he'd have liked to pursue the topic, he knew better than to push it. He kissed her good night. "Okay."

Replaying the conversation in his mind, he frowned. Did Jennifer see Anna as some sort of threat? If so, what was he supposed to do about it?

Not for the first time, he felt like he was in over his head with Jennifer and Chad. Just when he thought he had things pretty much figured out, one of them did something to throw him for a loop and he realized he'd been fooling himself.

Anna checked her purse for the third time. The money *had* to be there. It had slipped behind the lining, she told herself. Painstakingly, she removed everything and dumped the purse upside down.

Nothing.

She didn't like what she was thinking.

Suspecting her brother of stealing from her left her feeling like the lowest form of humanity. But if Jeff didn't take it, where was the money?

Mentally she retraced her route home from the bank. A stop by the dry cleaners, a quick trip to the grocery store, and then home. No, the hundred dollars had been in her purse when she'd walked in the door. Now it was gone.

Her head began to pound with a dull throb. She massaged her temples, giving up when she discovered the motion only intensified the pain.

Should she confront Jeff or pretend she didn't miss the money? Honesty demanded that she confront him, but she shrank from it. What if she drove him away with her suspicions?

Hard on the heels of that came an unsettling thought. If Brady were here, he'd know what to do. She dismissed the idea as quickly as it had appeared. Family problems were meant to stay in the family. Period.

Besides, how did she tell someone that she suspected her own brother of stealing from her? She could barely frame the words in her mind, much less voice them aloud. Giving voice to them would lend them that much more credence.

In the end, she did what she knew she had to.

"You're accusing me of stealing money from you?" Jeff asked, his voice shrill with indignation when she asked him about it over dinner.

"I'm asking you," she corrected. "I had a hundred dollars in my purse when I came home from the bank. Now it's gone."

"Maybe you didn't take as much out at the bank as you thought," he offered. "Or you might have spent more at the store than you thought. You know how you're always saying that it's easy to spend fifty dollars when you only meant to spend ten."

A cajoling note had entered his voice. Usually, Anna was powerless to resist him when he smiled at her, but this time was different.

"You don't know how much I wish that was true."

"Why won't you believe it?"

"Because it's not true. The money was in my purse. It's not there now." She reached for his hand, but he pulled away from her. "If you needed it, you had only to tell me."

"I told you. I didn't take it." But his gaze shifted away from hers.

"I don't understand, Jeff. We used to be so close. Especially after Mom died. Now I feel I hardly know you."

"You don't know me!" He pushed his chair back from the table and stormed from the house.

Anna looked at the denim jacket thrown across the sofa. Hating herself for doing it, she picked it up and searched the pockets. She wasn't sure whether she was relieved or disappointed when she found only a couple of dollars and change.

Hoping to ease the tension, she made Jeff's favorite brownies with cream cheese frosting for dessert that night.

He looked at the peace offering and gave a nasty smile. "You know something, Sis? Brownies don't cut it anymore. I'm seventeen. Not seven. Why don't you give them to your boyfriend? Or is he interested in something else?"

More angry than she'd ever been in her life, she slapped her brother. She watched in horror as a red stain spread over his cheek. She started to reach out to him, then dropped her hand at the expression on his face. "I'm sorry."

"Don't be. Now I don't have to feel guilty anymore." Despite his earlier words, he picked up a couple of brownies, stuffed them into his pocket, and took the stairs two at a time.

She heard the slam of a door and knew she'd lost him.

When she knocked at his door later that night, the only response was silence. She tried pushing it open only to find it locked.

"Jeff?"

"Yeah?"

"Please, let me in."

"What's the matter? Do you want to search my room?"

Anna could feel her face heat up as she acknowledged that she'd actually thought of it. "I just want to talk."

"Well, I don't feel like talking. Leave me alone."

She never felt more alone than she did now, not even after her mother had died. At least then she and Jeff had had each other. She stared at the door, willing it to open. But it remained stubbornly shut.

Unable to do anything more, she went to her own room and got ready for bed. Normally, she enjoyed the crisp coolness of the sheets against her skin. She barely noticed it tonight, her emotions still tangled in knots over the fight with Jeff.

Sleep eluded her as she replayed the conversation with her brother over and over in her mind. What could she have done differently? The question taunted her. A tear rolled down her cheek as she tried to accept what she already knew. She'd lost Jeff.

She slipped into sleep just as night slipped quietly into day.

Pink sunlight edged around the bedroom curtains, spilling across the bedspread with a rainbow of color. She watched the shifting colors, smiling at the way they appeared to chase each other. Picnics deserved light and laughter. Nature promised to provide the first; she hoped she could summon the second.

Her smile dwindled as she remembered last night.

Today she longed to forget about everything but being with Brady.

"Anna, can I have another piece? Please?" Chad held out his plate with a look of such hopeful expectancy that she couldn't refuse.

"Sure." She cut a huge piece of chocolate cake and placed it on his plate.

"If he has a stomachache in the middle of the night, I'm calling you," Brady warned. "That's his third piece."

"I know. But he said it was the best cake

in the whole world. No woman can resist that kind of praise. Besides, he ate all his salad."

"Well, that makes it all right then," he teased. He touched a finger to her mouth. "Chocolate icing," he said gravely.

"Oh."

He licked his finger. "Chad's right. Best cake in the whole world."

"Is that why you had two pieces?"

"One and a half. Jennifer got the other half."

"Uh-huh," she said, gathering up the dirty plates. "Then why did I see you helping yourself to her piece?"

He held up his hands. "I admit it. I'm a closet chocoholic. I snitched her cake when she couldn't finish it."

"You'd think you'd never seen chocolate cake before."

"Not like that I haven't." He took a plate from her hands. "Why don't we relax while the kids are playing? Come on, I want to show you something."

They hiked up a trail that led to a lookout point. The valley below spread before them with panoramic splendor. Green pastures were pieced together like a patchwork quilt edged with dark furrows. Fields of wheat were golden ribbons crisscrossing the landscape. Overhead, an eagle soared.

"Ever been here before?" Brady asked.

"There was never much time for . . ." she spread her hands, ". . . things like this when I was growing up."

Glad he'd been the one to show it to her, Brady pulled her closer, draping an arm around her shoulders.

"It's beautiful," she said.

Looking at her, he agreed. "Beautiful."

The light played tricks with her hair, weaving strands of red and honey through it. Gold-tipped eyelashes framed eyes so blue they rivaled the sky. Freckles dusted her nose, tempting him to kiss each one. His gaze dropped to her mouth.

The kiss that followed matched the setting. Natural. Simple. She tasted of sunlight and chocolate. The combination was a heady one, and Brady caught his breath as his lips found hers once more.

This time her lips parted beneath his, and he tasted the sweetness he knew was hers alone.

When he released her, he heard her soft sigh and knew she'd been as affected as he was. His own breath came in ragged bursts.

Anna looked up at him with confused eyes. "I . . . You . . ."

"It surprised me too," he said. He didn't attempt to kiss her again. She wasn't ready for it. Neither was he. He needed time to adjust to the rush of feelings that threatened to overtake him.

She shielded her eyes against the glare of the sun. Or was it to avoid looking at him? "We'd better get back to Jennifer and Chad."

The reluctance he heard in her voice matched his own. He wanted to spend time with her, here where the mountains touched the sky and the air smelled of pine and earth. It felt right that they should share this place together. It felt more than right.

"The children . . ."

She was right. But he was reluctant to leave this spot, to break the spell of its enchantment.

"Glad you came?" he asked as he helped her over a rough patch of ground.

"How could I not be? The day's been perfect. I wish . . ."

"What, Anna? What do you wish?"

"That it didn't have to end. That it could go on forever."

Her honesty touched him, much more than could anything more eloquent. "I do too. But it doesn't have to be the end. There'll be other —"

She put a finger to his lips. "Don't. Don't promise the future. Today's enough."

He saw the sadness hinted at in her eyes and guessed at its cause.

Jeff.

"The day's not over yet," he said and caught her hand.

She looked startled and then smiled. "No, it's not." After that, she seemed determined to shake off her earlier melancholy and laughed as they scampered down the path.

They were breathless when they reached the meadow.

"Hey, Uncle Brady, Anna. Where did you two go?" Chad asked. "We want to play Frisbee." He threw back his arm and let the red plastic disc fly. "Catch!"

Brady intercepted the Frisbee as it arced toward him. With a flick of the wrist, he spun it to Jennifer. The four of them tossed it back and forth, Brady and Anna laughing like children as they ran to keep up with Chad and Jennifer.

After an hour, Brady dropped to the ground, pulling Anna down with him. "Enough," he said, panting heavily.

"You guys aren't quitting already, are you?" Chad asked. "We're just getting started."

"Give us old folk a chance to catch our breath." Brady winked at Anna. "Maybe a piece of chocolate cake would revive me."

She poked his arm good-naturedly. "Any more cake and you won't be able to move at all."

"I thought you were on my side," he grumbled. But he stood, pulling her up with him.

"I am. That's why I'm not letting you have any more cake. Come on, Jennifer, let's show these men how Frisbee's supposed to be played."

Brady wondered if he was the only one to notice Jennifer's hesitation.

Anna tossed the disc at Jennifer and grinned as Brady leaped to grab it, only to fall on his rear.

"Okay, so you want to play rough?" He pulled Chad to one side. "Strategy meeting," he announced grandly.

He flicked the Frisbee to Chad who caught it easily and ran with it.

"Hey, no fair," Jennifer yelled, chasing after her brother.

"That was a sneaky trick," Anna said as she watched the kids race across the meadow.

"Yeah. Wasn't it?" He caught her hand and pulled her down on the grass.

The sun-dried grass whispered its protest as he lay down beside her. He inhaled deeply of the sweet aroma that filled his senses.

"You smell like wildflowers." He tucked a strand of her hair behind her ear. "I couldn't go home without doing this once more." He closed his lips over hers.

When the kiss ended, she looked at him with bemused eyes.

She started to speak, but he put a finger to her mouth. "Don't. Don't say anything right now. Just know that I care about you. Very much."

"Brady . . ."

"I know, sweetheart. I know."

"How do you know what I was going to say?"

"You were about to tell me all the reasons we shouldn't be together."

She looked away. "How did you know?"

"Because I know you." He traced the line of her jaw. "I won't promise not to rush you, Anna. But I'll be patient for as long as I can."

"That's all I ask."

His hand slipped behind her neck to arch her to him. His lips hovered over hers.

"Are you two kissing again?" Jennifer asked, startling both of them with her return.

Self-consciously, they pushed apart.

Brady ruffled his niece's hair, disturbed by the accusation he heard in her voice. "Sometimes, when adults like each other, they kiss."

"I know that," Chad said importantly, joining them. "That's what my friend Jason's parents do. He told me."

Jennifer glared at her brother. "They're married. Anna and Uncle Brady aren't married. They aren't supposed to kiss and stuff like that."

Another complication, Brady thought, and expelled a long breath. "Come on, gang. It's four o'clock. I have to be on duty in another two hours."

"Can we do this again? Real soon?" Chad asked.

Brady looked at Anna. "What about you? Are you up to another day with these urchins?"

She made a face at him. "Do I get a chance to rest up first?"

"Only if you promise to come."

She put out her hand, which he took solemnly. "You're on."

"Great!" Chad whooped.

Jennifer remained conspicuously silent. Brady and Anna exchanged glances over the girl's head.

Quietly, they gathered up the remains of

the picnic and loaded the car. Brady started the car and headed down the mountain. First Chad, then Jennifer, dropped off to sleep, their gentle snoring a soft counterpoint to the noise of the engine.

Jennifer's attitude troubled him. Something was bothering her. Something concerning Anna.

"Jennifer's upset," Anna said, echoing his own thoughts. "She's jealous."

Jealous. He hadn't thought of that, but he realized Anna was probably right.

"I'm afraid you're right. I don't understand it. I know she likes you."

"She's afraid you and I . . ."

He gave a rueful smile. "I guess I've been pretty obvious." He slanted a questioning look at her. "How do you feel about it?"

"I'm sorry she's upset."

"That's not what I mean. How do you feel about us?"

"I like you, Brady. A lot."

He heard the hesitation in her voice.

"It's okay, sweetheart. I promised I'm not going to rush you." He squeezed her hand. "And don't worry about Jennifer. She'll come around."

"I hope so," she said doubtfully.

So do I.

As Brady pulled up at Anna's house he leaned over to touch his lips to hers. "Thank you for coming today."

"I enjoyed it."

"So did I."

He gave in to the temptation to kiss her once more. This time he didn't brush his lips across hers with a light caress. He kissed her fully.

When he lifted his head he saw how deeply she'd been affected and allowed himself to hope that there was a future for them.

Anna let herself out of the car. "Thanks for . . . everything." The little hitch in her voice snagged his emotions, as did the haste with which she started to the house. She was clearly anxious to put some distance between them.

"Anna, wait."

But she'd already let herself into the house. Brady turned, deciding it was for the best. They both needed time to adjust to what was happening between them. He started to turn the ignition key when he saw Anna running toward him.

He jumped out of the car. "What is it?"

She shoved a piece of paper toward him. "Jeff's gone."

CHAPTER EIGHT

Brady took the note and scanned it quickly. "Has he done this before?"

She shook her head. "He's threatened to, but he's never actually done it." Her voice trembled and she fought to bring it under control and concentrate on what Brady was saying.

"Where would he go?"

"I don't know."

Gently, he pushed her into a chair. "Does he have any friends he might spend the night with? Sometimes it's as simple as that. A kid gets mad, decides he's going to teach his parents a lesson, and bunks with a friend. In the morning he comes home and everything's fine."

"I wish I could believe that."

"What do you know about Jeff's friends?"

"Not much," she admitted. "He's pretty closemouthed about his friends these days." Could there be any greater torture than waiting and not knowing?

Jeff, where are you?

She started calling. Each time, the answer was the same. No, Jeff isn't here. Yes, we'll call if we see him.

Two hours later, she buried her face in her hands. If Jeff had left for good, it was her fault. She'd driven him away with her suspicions.

The hours stretched before her. She prayed that Jeff would return, but the unrelenting silence mocked her.

When the call came, she grabbed for the phone.

"Oh, Brady, it's you. I hoped it was Jeff."

"I'm sorry. Still no word?"

"No. Nothing." Her voice broke on the last word, and she stifled a sob. "I called everyone I could think of. No one's seen him." She hesitated. "Could you do something?"

"It's too early for a missing persons report," he said. "But I can put out a description, unofficially. We might turn up something."

She knew she was asking more than she had a right to, more than she should. But it was her brother. If Brady could help, she wouldn't — couldn't — deny Jeff that chance.

Two hours later, the phone jarred her awake.

"Anna, we've found him."

"Where? How did you —"

"Meet me at the hospital."

"The hospital? Is he hurt?"

Brady hesitated. "No. But he's hurting." With that he hung up.

She dressed in record time and broke every speed limit in the city on the drive to the hospital. She found Brady in the emergency room. "Brady, where is —"

"A doctor's with him. He's treating Jeff for narcotics abuse."

"Jeff doesn't use drugs."

"When someone is taking drugs, the family is often the last to know. It's not just marijuana. I'm afraid he's graduated to something a lot stronger."

She pulled away from him. "You're wrong. I'd know if he were doing something like that."

Brady shook his head. "Honey, he's been on drugs for months. You just didn't see it."

Her chin lifted in unconscious challenge. "You're wrong. You have to be."

He put his hands on her shoulders. "Jeff needs help, Anna. If you won't believe me, at least talk to the doctor."

She raised her gaze to his and knew he

was telling her the truth. Why hadn't she seen it before?

The doctor appeared then. "Ms. Lancaster?"

She nodded. "Can I see my brother now?"

"He's sedated. He won't be able to see anyone for the next few hours. I suggest you go home and get some sleep."

She looked at him blankly. "I have to wait for Jeff. I have to be here when he wakes up."

Brady signaled to the doctor, who discreetly disappeared. Taking her hand, Brady led her to a cracked vinyl couch. "Anna, Jeff's stoned out of his mind. He won't be waking up for a long time. Right now, you need to rest."

She shook off his hand. "I can't leave without Jeff. I won't leave."

"Jeff needs help. Professional help."

"Then I'll help him. I'll drop all my students for the rest of the summer. I'll be there more for him. If I weren't working so much, this wouldn't have happened. He's just seventeen," she added defensively.

"Jeff's not a child. In six months, he'll be eighteen. If he screws up then, he can be tried as an adult. The judges won't be sympathetic anymore. There'll be no more suspended sentences. And he won't go to juvenile hall. It'll be jail. Do you know what happens to a kid in jail?" His voice softened. "You can't take responsibility for him forever."

"I'm not trying to take responsibility." Exhaustion and fear exacted their price and she turned on him. "Jeff lost his father and his mother. Doesn't that entitle him to a bit of compassion?"

"What about you? You lost your parents too. I don't see you drowning your troubles in a shot of coke."

"You've got it all figured out, haven't you? Brady Matthews, cop extraordinaire, devoted uncle. Well, maybe some of us aren't so *together* as you, Detective Matthews. Some of us need some help along the way."

He gave her a long look, one that caused her to drop her gaze in shame. Brady hadn't deserved that kind of outburst. He'd only tried to help, and she'd thrown that back in his face.

"Then see that he gets that help. The kind professionals are trained to give."

Anna watched him walk away. She wanted to call him back, to tell him she was sorry. But she couldn't. Not now. Not until she had time to understand what was happening to Jeff and to her.

She stared at the scarred tile floor, yellowed and cracked with years of use. The squares blurred and she shook her head, trying to shake off the waves of exhaustion that washed over her. More weary than she could ever remember, she sank onto the couch. Valiantly, she tried to remain alert, but her eyes drifted shut.

She was dreaming. Brady was there and so was Jeff. Each was beckoning to her. When she started toward one, the other called her back. Torn between the two, she felt herself yanked in first one direction, then the other.

When a nurse touched Anna's shoulder, she jerked awake. "Jeff, where is —"

"If you'll follow me."

She followed the nurse through a maze of corridors until they came to a small room. Anna knocked softly before pushing open the door.

"Jeff?"

"Hi, Sis."

He was pale, his skin only a fraction of a shade darker than the hospital-white sheet.

She roused a smile. "How're you feeling?"

"All right. No big deal."

His pathetic attempt to dismiss what had

happened effectively destroyed what little composure she had left.

"So what's new?" he asked.

What's new is that you're in a hospital after a drug overdose and I'm scared to death. But she couldn't tell him that. She hunted for something to say, anything but what was really on her mind.

"The doctor says you can come home tomorrow."

"Great. The food here stinks and the nurse looks like something from the black lagoon."

She couldn't summon a smile at his exaggerations and pleated the sheet between her fingers. "Jeff, the doctor thinks that you need help. Professional help."

"He's an old woman. Just get me out of here, Sis. I'll lay off junk. I promise."

She wanted to believe him. She ached to believe him. "He suggested several treatment centers. Places where you can get the kind of help you need."

"Hey, I can quit anytime I want. I just needed something last night, you know?"

"No, I don't know," she said honestly.

"You wouldn't," he muttered.

"What do you mean?"

"Nothing." He turned away. "Look, I'm wiped out. Can we talk later?"

"Sure." Uncertainly, she touched his shoulder. "I'll be back tonight. Okay?"

"Yeah. Just leave me alone right now, will you?"

Outside, she shielded her eyes against the glare of the sun and started toward her car.

Another car pulled up beside her. Brady opened a door. "Had any breakfast?"

He looked so good, she couldn't help the smile that crept past the tiredness and anxiety. "No."

"Hop in."

"My car —"

"We'll pick it up later. Come on." She hesitated. "You probably haven't eaten since last night," he said as she slid in beside him.

She nodded reluctantly.

"Hungry?"

"Starved," she confessed. She watched as he turned north onto the freeway. "Where're we going?"

"Ogden. I know a health food place that makes great pita sandwiches."

"I thought you said breakfast."

"Have you checked the time?"

She looked at her watch. Eleven o'clock in the morning. "Aren't you supposed to be at work?"

"I've got some days off due me. I decided to take one." Gently, he pushed her back against the seat. "Lay back and close your eyes. We'll be there soon."

She did as he suggested.

The rest did her good. She awoke, feeling more rested than she'd believed possible.

"Are we in Ogden yet?"

Brady slanted a smile at her. "We passed Ogden a couple of hours ago."

She sat up straight and looked at the passing scenery. They were climbing, the car pulling against the steep grade of the road.

"Why didn't you wake me up?"

"You were sleeping so peacefully that I couldn't. Angry?"

A reluctant smile touched her lips. "How could I be?"

"Good. We'll be there in half an hour."

"Where's there?"

"You'll see."

Knowing she wasn't going to get any more information from him, she sank back into the seat and let her mind wander. Predictably, it settled on Jeff. She was still struggling to accept the fact that Jeff had been taking drugs.

The personality changes, new friends, always short of money — all were classic signs of drug abuse. Why hadn't she seen them before?

Because she hadn't wanted to look. Or she'd been too wrapped up in her own problems — namely how to keep a roof over their heads — to notice what was happening.

Neither answer excused her, and she slumped lower into the seat. Brady had seen what was happening. If she'd listened to him, if she hadn't closed her eyes to what was so obvious now . . .

A hand closed around hers. "Cut it out. It's not your fault."

She looked up. "How did you know?"

"Because I know you. You were blaming yourself for Jeff's problems. It won't wash, Anna. Sometime, Jeff has to start taking responsibility for himself."

"Seems like we've had this conversation before."

"Maybe this time you'll listen."

"Maybe this time I will," she said slowly. For the first time, she seriously considered what Brady had said. Had she assumed too much responsibility for Jeff?

"We're there," Brady announced, bringing the car to a halt. He let himself out and then opened her door.

Anna looked around in pleasure. Stately pines towered over them, providing an impressive backdrop for the cabin tucked into the mountainside. A soft breeze cooled the air and Anna shivered.

"Let's go inside," Brady said, taking her arm to help her over the rough patches of ground.

The cabin's interior was a delight. Hand-woven rugs brightened plank floors. Log and plaster walls gave a rustic air to the place. Simple pine furniture completed the look.

"Is it yours?" she asked, gesturing around her.

"I bought the land a while back and worked on the cabin whenever I could. I finished it last year. It's not fancy, but I like it."

"It's perfect," she said, more impressed than ever to learn that he'd built it himself. "I bet the kids love it."

Brady grinned. "If they had their way, we'd be living up here. Do you want the grand tour now or after lunch?"

"Now, definitely."

He showed her the compact but fully equipped kitchen. A ladder led to a loft which held two bedrooms and a bathroom. Each room reflected the same homey air that characterized the main floor of the cabin.

Back in the kitchen, Brady rummaged through the cabinets and produced a couple of cans.

"What can I do to help?" she asked.

"Nothing. Just keep me company while I heat this up."

She watched as he stirred together ingredients, added a few spices, and heated the mixture on the stove.

Fifteen minutes later they sat down at the trestle table. "I'm not promising what this tastes like," Brady warned as he spooned a combination of beans and vegetables onto her plate.

Anna took a bite. "It's delicious. How did you get to be such a good cook?"

"It was either that or starve. Eating in restaurants gets old after a while. Especially if you're by yourself."

They finished the simple meal and cleaned up the dishes. Anna took another look around the cabin. It said a lot about its owner, reminding her that Brady was a complex man.

He came to stand behind her, linking his hands around her waist. "We'll come again," he said, "and bring Chad and Jennifer."

"I'd like that."

Neither felt inclined to talk during the trip back to Salt Lake. Anna appreciated the companionable silence; she had a lot of thinking to do.

By the time they reached the city, dusk had settled, softening the harsh edges of the mountains and streaking the sky with color.

The time away had allowed Anna to see what she had to do. She laid her hand on Brady's arm. "Thank you. For everything."

"You're welcome."

"Would you do one more thing for me?"

"Name it."

"Drop me at the hospital."

"Sure." He switched lanes. "What are you going to do?"

"Something I should have done a long time ago."

Jeff was awake, edgy, and anxious to be released when she knocked at his door. "Get me out of here," he said.

"The doctor said tomorrow," Anna reminded him. "Right now, I want to talk."

"I don't feel like it."

"What you feel like doesn't matter."

She felt his surprise. She'd never talked to him like that before. Another mistake.

"Why, Jeff?"

"Why what?"

She gestured around her. "Why did you do this to yourself?"

He glared at her. "Because I wanted something for me. Something you'd never done."

"Something I'd never done?"

"Yeah. Perfect Anna would never take drugs, never get into trouble."

"So you took drugs because I'd never done it?" She couldn't keep the horror from her voice.

He shrugged. "Is that so hard to believe?"

She didn't have an answer for that.

"You always had it together. Always the perfect student, the perfect daughter, the perfect everything. Do you know how sick I got of Mom asking me why couldn't I be more like you?"

She drew back, stung by the venom in his voice. "Why didn't you say something?"

"There wasn't any point. She was right. You were perfect. I wasn't."

"Mom loved you."

"Yeah? Then why was she always on my back?"

"Because she wanted the best for you. Just like I do."

Just like I do. The words stuck in her

throat. Had she tried to act like Jeff's mother, instead of his sister? Is that what Brady had been trying to tell her?

"Mom loved you, Jeff," she repeated.

"Maybe. It doesn't matter any more."

"It matters. Can't you see what you're doing? You're trying to get back at her — and at me — by hurting yourself."

She was doing it again. Confusing herself with her mother. Anna studied her brother. Had he resented her interference? Had he seen it as yet one more piece of evidence that he didn't measure up?

"Jeff, we both need help. The doctor —"

"Can it wait? All I want right now is to sleep for two weeks."

She looked at his wan face and nodded. "We'll talk more tomorrow."

"Yeah. Tomorrow."

Anna spent the morning cleaning. She recognized her burst of energy for what it was. Scrubbing cabinets and mopping floors kept her too busy to think.

At the hospital, she found a new flower arrangement.

"The cop sent it," Jeff said carelessly.

"Maybe you can thank him tonight." Anna started gathering up clothes and putting them in the small suitcase she'd brought with her.

Jeff snatched a shirt from her. "I can do it."

"I know. I was just trying to help."

"That's the problem. You're always trying to help."

"I'm sorry."

"Yeah. Look, can we get out of here? This place gives me the creeps."

Once they were home, Jeff headed to his room. Anna blocked his way. "We need to talk."

"Later."

"No, Jeff. Not this time." Anna waited until Jeff sat down on the sofa. "You need help, Jeff. More help than I can give."

"I experimented with some coke. No big deal."

"You could have died."

"I didn't."

She took a breath and tried again. "Brady gave me the names of some treatment centers. I thought —"

"I don't need you thinking for me." When she remained silent, Jeff stood up and started to pace. "I'm not an addict. I did something dumb. It won't happen again."

More than anything, she wanted to believe him.

"I told you the truth," Jeff mumbled.

"Have you?"

He avoided her gaze. "Sure I have." Cheeks mottled and hands clenched, he looked so guilty that, if the situation were less serious, she'd have laughed.

"I wish I could believe you."

"Why don't you?" Without giving her a chance to reply, he answered for her. "It's because of your cop boyfriend, isn't it? He's convinced you that I'm no good."

"I thought you liked the idea of my cop boyfriend."

"That was before," he muttered.

"When you figured he could be useful."

"What's the big deal? We use people all the time. I do. Even you."

"I don't use people."

"How about when you asked Matthews to help find me?" he challenged. "You're saying you didn't use him then?"

Direct hit. Dark color suffused her face as she remembered how she'd asked, begged Brady to help her find Jeff.

"You're right. I did use him. I'm not very proud of it."

"So it's all right for you to use people, but not for me. Right?"

"No. It's never right to use someone else."

"I made a few mistakes. But I'm out of it now. Why don't you believe me?"

I want to. A part of her ached to believe her brother, but another part forced her to admit that he was still lying to her.

"I'm sorry, Jeff. I'm not bailing you out of any more trouble."

"Fine. I don't need you to baby-sit me. I never did."

It was the hardest thing she'd had to do, but she turned her back on him and walked away.

In her room, she sank onto her bed and cried. Fear mingled with pain until she no longer knew which was stronger. Exhausted and sick at heart, she slept.

It was there that Brady found her, huddled on her bed.

She looked so vulnerable that he hesitated to wake her. When a knock at the door elicited no response, he tested it and found it open. Walking inside, he called her name. Alarmed, he climbed the stairs to find her in the bedroom, lying on her bed.

He brushed the hair back from her face and saw the ravages of tears. She stirred but didn't waken.

Brady covered her with a quilt, brushed a kiss over her lips, and closed the door behind him.

Downstairs, he began preparing dinner.

The cupboards yielded a package of spaghetti, tomato sauce, and spices.

He didn't need to ask what had upset her. The answer was obvious.

Anna woke to the enticing aroma of simmering tomatoes and spices. She frowned when she noticed the quilt that covered her. Had Jeff . . . ? Answering her own question, she shook her head. After splashing water on her face, she ventured downstairs.

"Hi, sleepyhead," Brady called cheerfully from where he stirred a pot of something at the stove.

"Hi." A smile curved her lips as she took in the picture of Brady Matthews, police detective, decked out in a frilly apron. He should have looked ridiculous. But the apron, stretched tautly across his chest, only enhanced his appeal.

"Supper will be ready in a minute," he said, and pulled out a chair for her.

She sat down and wondered if she'd just wandered through Alice's looking glass. "When did you get here?"

"About an hour ago. You were sleeping so peacefully, I decided not to wake you." He threw her a teasing smile. "You were snoring like a steam engine."

"I never snore."

"Okay. You don't snore. But something was sure puffing away."

"Well, it wasn't me."

"Sure it wasn't."

The silly exchange eased her embarrassment, and she was able to do justice to the meal.

By the time they'd finished the spaghetti and salad, she felt up to the questions she was sure were coming.

"Feel like talking about it?" Brady asked.

"I don't know."

"Try me. Sometimes talking it through can help."

"What are you? Analyst, chef, or cop?"

"Just a friend," he said quietly, and took her hand to lead her into the living room.

Fifteen minutes later, he was shaking his head. "I hope you're right," he said when she told him that Jeff promised he was through with drugs. "I'd feel a lot better if he agreed to have some kind of counseling."

"So would I." She paused. "Did you . . . did you see him?"

"No. He was gone when I got here."

She'd expected as much. She had one more thing to clear up with Brady. "There's something else I have to tell you."

"What is it?" he asked when she hesitated. "Are you going to confess to robbing a bank?"

His teasing failed to rouse a smile. "Hey, it can't be as bad as all that."

"I'm afraid it is." She took a deep breath. "I used you when I asked you to help me look for Jeff. I'm sorry. I shouldn't have done it. I was just so worried."

He held up a hand. "You've got nothing to feel bad about. I'd have done the same for anyone."

"It was wrong, taking advantage of our relationship."

"It was human," he said, fitting a finger under her chin to lift her head so that their gazes met. "I didn't mind. I *wanted* to help you find Jeff."

"But I mind." She reached up to touch her lips to his. "You're a nice man."

"No, I'm not. I'm just a guy who happens to be crazy about you." He leered suggestively. "Think it'll do me any good?"

"You never know."

"In that case, I'll do the dishes. I wield a mean dishtowel."

"You cooked. You don't have to do the dishes too."

"You've had a rough day. Sit back and talk to me. I'll have this place cleaned up in no time."

Brady was smiling as he drove home. Being with Anna was like discovering that he believed in Santa Claus, the tooth fairy, and the Easter Bunny all over again. Even as worried as she was over Jeff, she managed to make him forget the ugliness he saw each day and to remember the reason why he'd decided to become a cop in the first place.

She asked about his job and then actually listened when he told her about it. She didn't flinch away from the ugly parts. Instead, she squeezed his hand, telling him she understood.

Anna wasn't like the other women he'd dated, who'd shied away from unpleasantness. She accepted his job as part of who he was.

She was worth risking his heart for.

He'd made one mistake — a big one — when he'd become involved with a woman who refused to understand what his job meant to him, but he wasn't about to compound it by letting Anna go. She meant too much to him.

The urge to tell her how he felt was almost overwhelming. Though he longed to share her responsibilities, he knew she'd refuse to listen to him until she believed Jeff was all right.

A frown creased his forehead as he thought about Jeff. Unless he could find a way to help her brother, Brady feared he and Anna stood little chance of a future together.

CHAPTER NINE

"The precinct's having a fourth of July carnival this Saturday," Brady said.

"Wow!" Chad said. "Can we stay all day?"

"We'll make a day of it. There's even a baseball game."

"Will there be anything to eat?"

Brady's laugh rumbled from deep inside him. His nephew had a one track mind. "Hot dogs, cotton candy, snow cones. And every other kind of junk food you can think of."

"Wow," Chad repeated. A worried frown replaced his smile. "Will you help me with my catching before then? I don't catch so good," he confided.

Brady smothered a smile. "Want to know a secret? I didn't catch so good when I was your age either. Maybe the problem's your mitt. How 'bout you and I go shopping for a new mitt?"

"Right now?"

"Whoa, partner. We haven't even asked Jennifer if she wants to go to the picnic yet."

"Will it be just us?" she asked, not looking at him.

"You, Chad, and me. And Anna if she can make it."

"You promised that the next time it'd be just us," she said, the pout in her voice matching the one on her lips.

"Chad, would you let me talk with Jennifer alone?"

"But —"

"Please."

Brady waited until his nephew was out of the room before turning back to Jennifer. "What's the matter, honey?"

"It's *her*. She's always butting in where she's not wanted."

"Anna?"

Jennifer nodded. "It used to be just you, me, and Chad. Now you always want to drag her along. She even went to the movies with us."

Brady did a mental replay of the night he'd asked Anna to join them to see a family film. Now that he thought about it, Jennifer had been more subdued than normal.

"Didn't you like having Anna there?"

Jennifer squirmed uncomfortably. "Sure. Especially when it got sort of scary. But I don't want her to come to the policeman's picnic with us. That's for families. You promised it'd be just the three of us."

Brady heard the accusation in her voice. "That was before I met Anna. I thought you liked her."

"I did. When she was my teacher. But I don't anymore. She's not my mother."

So that was it. "She's not trying to take your mother's place. No one could do that."

Jennifer sniffled. "Then why's she always hanging around? Sally told me that after her parents got divorced, her father married his girlfriend. Now he doesn't have time for her anymore."

"And you're afraid that if I marry Anna, that I won't have time for you and Chad? Is that it?" He drew her into his arms. "Don't you know I'll always have time for you? You're my best girl. Nothing's going to change that."

She pushed away from him. "What if you and Anna have a baby of your own? He'd be yours for real. You won't want Chad and me then." Tears sprang to her eyes. She tried to knuckle them away, but Brady stilled her hand.

It hurt. Even after a year, she still didn't trust him. "You think I'd leave you and Chad?"

Jennifer stared at the floor. "It's not like you wanted us around. I heard you talking with your friend. You said you *had* to take care of us when Mom died."

He pushed aside the quick rush of guilt as he remembered the incident. It had taken place right after Chad and Jennifer had arrived, when Brady was still trying to deal with his own grief over Leigh's death and adjust to having two children become part of his life.

"You're right. I did say that, but that was before I knew how much I was going to like having you and Chad live with me." He paused, searching for the right words. "You're part of my life now. A permanent part. We're a family, Jennifer. You and Chad and me. Whether or not I find someone to marry, nothing's going to change that."

"Then why do you want Anna too? Families don't need outsiders."

"Anna's not an outsider. She makes me feel happy inside." He touched his heart. "Here."

"You said Chad and me do that."

"You do," he said. "But Anna makes me

a different kind of happy. The kind that a man feels for a woman."

"A different kind?"

"The kind a man feels for a woman he . . . cares about."

Jennifer wrapped her arms around herself. "I wish it could be the way it was, just you and me and Chad. We did everything together."

"I know, honey. But it can be just as good. Maybe even better if you let Anna be part of our lives. She loves you, you know."

"She's just saying that to get on your good side."

He cupped her chin, forcing her to look at him. "You know better than that. Anna's not like that."

Her lips trembled. "I know. But . . ."

"But what?"

"I'm scared. First Dad died, then Mom. If you go away too, me and Chad'll be alone. Again." Fat tears rolled down her cheek.

He pulled her to him and held her as she cried. "I'm not leaving you. That's a promise."

She pulled away to look at him. "Really?"

"Really."

"Uncle Brady, if you and Anna get married, and you do have a baby, then what?"

"Then you'll have a baby brother or sister. Wouldn't you like that?"

She seemed to think about it. "Maybe. But who'd take care of him? Sometimes babies cry. And need their diapers changed. Sarah said all her little brother does is spit up his milk and . . ."

Brady suppressed a laugh. "I think I get the picture. You're right — babies are a lot of work. We'd all have to pitch in to help out." Brady paused.

"Jennifer, I love you and Chad. If, someday, Anna and I decide to get married, we'll all be one family. When you love someone, it doesn't mean you stop loving other people. It only means you have more love to give. Do you understand?"

"I think so."

"Good. Because I wouldn't do anything if I thought it would hurt you or Chad. Okay?"

"Okay." She threw her arms around his waist. "I love you, Uncle Brady."

"And I love you, pumpkin. Don't ever forget that."

"I won't."

"Think about what I said about Anna. If you let her, she could be a good friend to you. That's all she wants."

Jennifer's brow puckered. "Maybe."

Brady dropped a kiss on her forehead. It was a start, he thought. He'd settle for that.

He repeated the conversation to Anna that night over dinner. Rather than being insulted, she was concerned for him and Jennifer. He should have known. Anna would always think of others before herself.

A frown wrinkled her forehead. "I should have seen it coming."

He covered her hand with his own. "Hey, don't blame yourself. Jennifer would have a problem with any woman right now."

She managed a shaky smile. "I just happened to be in the wrong place at the wrong time."

"Correction: you were in the *right* place at the *right* time. For me." His voice had turned low, its husky tones a gentle caress of her senses.

He skimmed her cheek, his calloused fingertips creating a pleasant friction against her skin. His gaze rested on her warmly, and she felt herself responding to it. But she pushed the feelings away. She had to if she were to help Brady solve the problem with Jennifer.

A frown creased her forehead as she looked at him. His face was seamed with lines, lines she suspected were caused by worry and fatigue. She longed to reach out and smooth them away but she forced her mind back to the matter at hand.

"How did Jennifer seem after you talked with her?"

"All right. But she's still worried that if you and I marry and have children, we won't want her and Chad anymore."

"That's ridiculous."

"That's what I told her."

The implication of his words sank in all at once. "I meant it's ridiculous that you and . . . that we . . ."

"Is it, Anna?"

She averted her gaze. "Of course it is. We've never talked — about that, I mean."

"Maybe it's time we did."

She tried to control her growing panic. She wasn't ready for this. Not yet. There were too many questions in her life right now and not nearly enough answers.

"I care about you, Brady." It was a lot more than caring, she acknowledged silently. But to share those feelings now wouldn't be fair, to herself or to Brady.

"Do I hear a 'but' in there somewhere?" he said.

A smile skimmed her lips. He was too perceptive. The smile dimmed as she said the words she had to. "It's Jeff. I can't leave him alone."

"No one's asking you to. He'd be part of our family. Just like Chad and Jennifer. I always wanted a big family. We'd just be getting a head start."

She reached up to kiss him. "Thank you."

"For what?"

"For being you."

"Did you honestly think I wouldn't want Jeff to live with us if we decided to get married?"

She hesitated. "A lot of people would say you'd be justified."

"What kind of man do you think I am?" He paused. "Was there someone else? Someone who refused to —"

"Take on a package deal?" she finished for him. "That was how Tom put it. He said he didn't need a ready-made family. Especially one that included a troublemaker like Jeff." She heard the bitterness coloring her voice and tried to control it. His rejection still hurt. Even after a year.

Brady swore softly.

"I'm sorry," she said. "I know you're not like Tom. But, in a lot of ways, he was right."

"He was a fool."

"No, just someone who knew what he wanted. Which wasn't Jeff and me."

"Tell me about him."

"We were engaged. After my mother died and he learned Jeff would be living with us, he gave me a choice. Jeff or him." She laughed hollowly.

"You're better off without him."

"That's what I told myself."

He tilted her chin up to touch her lips with his own. "I'll pick you up at nine Saturday morning."

"But —"

"No excuses allowed. We're spending the day together."

"What about Jennifer?"

"She'll come around. It won't do her — or us — any good if we ignore the problem. She'll get used to seeing us together. She has to. Until then I wonder if we should find her another tutor."

"I think that's a good idea," Anna agreed. It hurt that she wouldn't be able to continue teaching Jennifer, but the little girl's welfare was what mattered.

"You don't mind?"

"No, I don't mind. Jennifer needs help, if not from me, then from someone else." She hesitated. "About you and me —"

"I can wait." He pressed a kiss to her forehead. "As long as you know how I feel, I can wait."

I hope so, she thought after he'd left. No matter what Brady said, she couldn't ask him to take on Jeff's problems. She'd have to see this through on her own.

The fourth of July dawned clear and hot — perfect for a day at a carnival. Brady was determined to make it a day to remember. Especially for Anna.

He stole a look at her. Shadows still underscored her eyes, giving them a bruised look that touched his heart. Things were a long way from being settled with Jeff. She was going to forget about problems today, though, Brady promised himself.

Saffron fields of wheat shimmered under the heat of the July sun. Lazy clouds ambled across the sky. Prairie dogs ventured from their burrows, yipped shrilly, then scuttled deep into their tunnels.

Nature had done her part. Now it was his turn.

Brady found himself turning to Anna for the sheer pleasure of looking at her. Hair tumbled about her face. Cheeks sun-kissed with freckles and lips innocent of makeup, she was the most beautiful woman he'd ever seen.

"Happy?"

He reached over to take her hand. She

didn't answer, he noted. But it was enough that she let her hand stay in his. "Are you glad you came?"

"How could I not be?"

He had had to listen closely to catch her reply.

"Hey, Uncle Brady, when do we get to eat?" Chad demanded from the back seat.

Brady grinned. *Some things never change.* "Soon," he promised.

"*How* soon?"

"As soon as we get there. Look kids, why don't you close your eyes? By the time you open them, we'll be there."

"We're not babies," Jennifer said in a cool voice.

Brady shared a look with Anna. *It'll be all right,* he tried to tell her with a quick squeeze of her hand.

The slight pressure on his hand told him she understood.

She'd always understand, Brady thought. No matter what the problem, Anna would face it with the quiet strength and compassion that were so much a part of her. He smiled. That was only one of the reasons he loved her.

"Look!" Chad shouted.

A hot air balloon swayed above the fairgrounds, its green and gold stripes a brilliant splash of color against the sky. Scores of police cars lined the street, an overflow from the parking lot.

Brady pulled the car in beside a police van. "Hey, not so fast," he called as Chad and Jennifer bolted from the car. He sighed as they continued their dash to the brightly striped tent.

He caught Anna's grin and gave a rueful one in return. "I'm sure glad they listen to me."

She started to help him with the picnic hamper when he caught her hands and brought them to his lips. Slowly, he kissed the ridge of her knuckles.

"You guys coming or what?" Chad had stopped long enough to turn around and shoot them an impatient look.

Brady's grin spread. "I always did have lousy timing."

"Your timing isn't lousy, just your choice of places," she said with a glance around them. "We'd better hurry up or Chad'll skin us alive."

The day was a kaleidoscope of color and sound, smell and taste. Anna wanted to sample it all. Even more, she wanted to do so with Brady. His hand rested on her waist, a sweet pressure that made her feel cherished. Just for today, she determined to put her troubles out of her mind.

At Chad's insistence, their first stop, after buying huge cones of cotton candy, was the shooting booth.

"Sorry," a young uniformed officer said to Chad. "You've got to be twelve or older."

"You do it, Uncle Brady," Chad said. "You're the best shot in the whole world."

Brady hefted the rifle, sighted it, and aimed.

Three direct hits.

"Congratulations, sergeant," the officer said and handed him a stuffed elephant.

Brady had already seen the way Jennifer's gaze had honed in on a floppy-eared elephant.

"Here you go," he said as he handed the improbably colored pink and purple elephant to his niece. "Won't he look nice on your bed?"

"It's a she," Jennifer said. "You can tell because she has a bow." She pointed to the pink ribbon that encircled the elephant's neck and then threw her arms around her uncle. "Thank you, Uncle Brady. She's beautiful."

Brady and Anna exchanged smiles over Jennifer's head.

Chad looked at the elephant in disgust.

"Elephants aren't pink and purple. They're gray." He tugged at Brady's hand. "Are we going to stand here all day looking at that stupid elephant or what?"

"Apologize to your sister," Brady said quietly.

"Sorry," Chad muttered. "But . . ." He looked at the carnival which sprawled in front of them. "I don't want to miss anything."

"Neither do I," Brady said and swung Chad up to settle him on his shoulders. "I know where there's a fishing pond that just happens to have a football."

"A football? In a pond?"

"You bet."

Anna smiled at the way Brady had deflected a potential problem. He was good with the kids, she thought. He may have been thrust into parenthood unprepared, but he was handling it better than most.

"Are you coming?" he asked when she lagged behind.

"I wouldn't miss it," she said, hurrying to catch up. "I've never seen a fishing pond that has footballs."

He steadied Chad with one hand while taking hers with the other. "Didn't I promise you a day you'd never forget?"

She nodded, feeling a catch in her

throat. It was all that and more.

At the fishing "pond," Brady helped Chad bait his line. "Okay, now throw your line over the side, and we'll see what you get."

With Chad's attention on his line, Anna slipped behind the partition and spotted the football. When the officer in charge of the booth started to reach for a toy camera, she handed him the ball. "This one," she mouthed.

"I got one, Uncle Brady. I got a football."

Chad's excited voice could be heard all over. The officer gave her a thumbs-up sign.

They spent the rest of the morning visiting booths, eating cotton candy, and devouring hot dogs. Even Jennifer appeared to be having a good time — until they reached the roller-coaster. She hung back.

"C'mon!" Chad shouted.

Brady looked at Anna. "Are you up to this?"

"Sure." She glanced at Jennifer. "You two go ahead. Jennifer and I'll be along in a minute."

"Can I ride with you?" Anna asked. "I don't know about you, but these things make me a little nervous."

Jennifer shrugged, but her gaze remained fixed on the roller-coaster. "I guess so."

The ride started off calmly enough. Then the roller-coaster started up an impossibly steep track, and Anna saw Jennifer tense. She reached for Anna during the drop, and Anna squeezed her hand. "It'll be over in a minute!" Anna shouted over the screams.

Jennifer's hand only tightened around Anna's. By the time the ride came to a stop, Jennifer was white-faced and shaking. "Don't tell them I was scared," she whispered.

Anna looked to the next car, where Brady and Chad were laughing, and then back to Jennifer. She brushed tears from the girl's cheek. "Want to know a secret?"

Jennifer managed a shaky nod.

"I was scared too."

Jennifer's giggle was the most beautiful sound Anna had heard in a long time. They unbuckled the safety belts and waited until Chad and Brady joined them.

"Did you girls have a good time?" Brady asked.

Jennifer and Anna shared a look. "The best," Jennifer said. "The absolute best."

Brady shot Anna a questioning look. *I'll tell you later,* her eyes promised.

The baseball game was girls against boys. Anna was grateful for another opportunity to build on the new beginning with the little girl. Maybe this time they'd be able to make it work.

When the girls' team won, Jennifer grabbed Anna around the waist. "We won! We won!"

She stayed at Anna's side for the rest of the day. Things weren't perfect yet, but they were a whole lot better than they had been, Anna thought on the drive home.

A whole lot better.

Some of her happiness dissolved as she thought about Jeff.

If only his problems were as easily solved.

CHAPTER TEN

"Brady, the lieutenant wants us in his office. Now." Jim glanced at the report Brady was typing and grinned slyly. "Unless you want to finish here."

Brady scowled at the manual typewriter which should have been labeled an antique years ago and donated to the Smithsonian. "I'd take stakeout duty for a month rather than do paperwork." He grabbed his jacket and shrugged it on. "Let's go."

The lieutenant was smiling, a bad sign in Brady's view. A smiling superior usually meant trouble. His boss leaned against the desk, his arms folded across his chest.

Brady wasn't fooled by the casual stance or the smile.

"Matthews, I understand you've been seeing Anna Lancaster."

Brady gave a cautious nod. "She tutors my niece.

"What do you know about her brother?"

"He's been in some trouble, the usual kid stuff."

"Do you know he hangs out with Mike Rafferty? The boys in Narcotics think Lancaster's helping Rafferty push dope to kids."

"How sure are they?"

"Enough to want to find out more. They've asked for our help."

Brady's face grew remote. He waited.

The lieutenant sighed heavily. "You're going to make me spell it out, aren't you. Okay, I will. They want you to find out if the Lancaster kid's involved. What he knows, who else is involved, the works."

"And how am I supposed to do that?"

"Any way you can."

"What way do you suggest, sir?"

"Can it, Matthews. You've got an in with the kid's sister. Use it."

Brady regarded his superior through half-closed eyes, his face mirroring none of his thoughts. "You mean use Anna."

The lieutenant frowned. "I mean find out what the sister knows. Maybe she can convince her brother to cooperate with us. If he helps us, chances are we can get him off with a light sentence. If not . . ."

"Why can't Narcotics use their usual snitches? Why go through the sister? She doesn't know anything. I'd stake my life on it."

"She may not know what's going on, but she might drop names, places where her brother hangs out. You know the drill."

"And if Jeff's clean?"

"If he is, there's no problem. Is there?"

Brady remained silent.

"Is there?" the lieutenant demanded.

"No, sir."

"Look, Matthews, I know you don't like this. I don't either. But we've got more junk reaching the streets every day. We've got to stop it. Any way we can."

Any way we can. The end justifies the means. Getting the job done no matter what the costs.

He'd heard it all before. He'd even believed it. But never before had the words twisted his gut as they did now.

"Do you have a problem with the assignment, Matthews?"

Yeah, I've got a problem, he wanted to shout. *I'm in love with the woman you want me to spy on.*

"Matthews?" the lieutenant prompted.

"No problem, sir."

"Good. Then get started. Davies here will back you up when you need it." He glanced at Davies, who nodded.

Back in his office, Brady ripped the report from the typewriter and crumpled it into a ball. Savagely, he slammed it against the wall.

Jim Davies stood at the door. "Mind if I come in?"

Brady shrugged. "Why not?"

Jim cocked a hip against the desk. "I know you feel like you got a raw deal. For what it's worth, I think so too."

Brady regarded him skeptically. "Yeah?"

"Yeah. But we're cops. So we do what we have to do."

"What we have to do stinks."

Jim grinned lazily. "You'll get no argument from me."

"So why do we keep doing it?"

"The big bucks we rake in every week."

Brady couldn't even dredge up a smile at the old joke.

The grin disappeared from Jim's face. "Because if we didn't, the creeps would take over. I'm not ready to turn the streets over to them. I don't think you are either."

"No matter who we end up hurting in the process."

Jim gave him a curious look. "How bad you got it for her?"

"Bad," Brady said. "Real bad. I was going to ask her to marry me. Now . . ."

He shoved a hand through his hair. "I don't know."

"That's rough."

"Look, Jim, I appreciate you coming here and everything. But I've got some thinking to do."

"Sure, I understand. If I can help . . ." Jim laid a hand on Brady's shoulder.

"Yeah, I know. Thanks."

Brady slumped over the desk and wondered why doing the right thing felt so wrong. For the first time since he'd become a cop, he considered another profession.

Heck, an insurance salesman sold policies, met his quotas, then went home to his wife and kids. He wasn't on call twenty-four hours a day, seven days a week, three hundred and sixty-five days a year. His personal life wasn't shot to pieces because of a job.

Brady tried to picture a nine-to-five job, safe and predictable, with weekends off and two weeks' paid vacation every year. There'd be a house in the suburbs, a station wagon in the driveway, and a big dog in the backyard. Try as he would, the image refused to take shape.

Muttering to himself, he picked up the crumpled report and tried to smooth away the wrinkles. He'd be darned if he was going to retype it.

For once he was grateful he wasn't seeing Anna tonight. She had a special tutoring session which would take up her whole evening. There was no way he could see her and pretend that everything was all right.

The following day he fought the urge to call her and cancel their date for that evening — an open-air concert at the park. His mouth twisted bitterly at his cowardice even as he acknowledged that there was no way he could *not* see her. Job aside, he wanted to see her; he needed to see her.

The reason was simple: he was in love with her.

In the end, he did what he'd known he would all along. That it was ripping the heart from him didn't — couldn't — matter.

He showed up at seven, holding a bouquet of daffodils. When he'd seen them in an outdoor market, he knew he had to get them. Their color, sunshine-bright and free of artifice, reminded him of Anna.

He handed them to her.

"What's the occasion?" she asked after thanking him.

"No occasion. They're a no-reason present."

"The best kind," she said, smiling.

He knew she was waiting for him to kiss her, and he complied. The quick peck on her cheek drew a surprised look from her, but she didn't comment on it.

She laced her fingers around his neck to draw him closer for a real kiss.

As soon as he could, he eased away. Kissing a source wasn't standard operational procedure. Kissing the woman he loved and intended to deceive — who he would undoubtedly hurt in the process — left him feeling all kinds of a louse.

He tried to ignore the hurt that clouded her eyes and forced a smile to his lips.

"Is anything wrong?" Anna asked.

"No," he said quickly. Too quickly. "What makes you ask?"

"I don't know. You look . . . distracted."

Some detective he was if he couldn't control his expression any better than that.

"Did something happen at the station?"

About to deny it, he changed his mind. "Yeah. You could say that. I got a new assignment." That much, at least, was the truth.

"Is it something you can talk about?"

He hesitated.

"If you'd rather not —"

"No, that's all right. I'd like to tell you about it." He sketched in the details of a robbery case, borrowing details from previous cases.

The lies left a sour taste on his lips. He resisted the urge to lick them clean, knowing he couldn't wipe away the taint of deceit. He waited, hoping she'd give him an opening, hoping she'd tell him to go home, hoping she'd do anything to take away the self-loathing that clung to him.

She brushed his cheek, her touch gentle as thistledown. "I wish I could help."

"I know."

Casually, ever so casually, he asked, "How's Jeff doing?"

He watched as Anna's smile dimmed. "All right, I guess. He's promised me he won't take anything again." He watched her face pale as if the memory hurt too much to put words to Jeff's drug use.

Brady knew just how much such promises were worth and ached for her, knowing that heartache was inevitable. But right now he had a job to do.

"He's out tonight," she said, her face brightening. "Applying for a job."

His interest pricked up. "At night?"

"It's a night watchman's job. With school out, I thought it was all right if he took a night job."

"Where at?"

She frowned. "I don't know. Someplace

downtown. Jeff was a little vague on the details."

He heard the defensiveness in her voice and knew he had to back off. Instead of frustration at not being able to follow the lead any further, he felt only relief.

It was short-lived, though. "Mike Rafferty suggested Jeff try for the job," Anna said.

"Rafferty?" He couldn't keep the scowl from his voice. "I thought Jeff wasn't seeing him anymore."

"I hoped he wouldn't. But he says Mike's trying to make a fresh start. I couldn't very well fault him for that. And when Mike came up with this job, well . . . maybe I was wrong about him."

"Yeah, maybe," Brady said, loving her even more.

Anna would always give someone the benefit of a doubt, even scum like Mike Rafferty.

"You're sure Jeff didn't say where this job is?"

She frowned. "Yes. I should have asked, but I didn't want to press him too much. You know how it is. Why all the questions?"

"Just curious," he said, hating the lie, hating himself for deceiving her. "If I knew where, maybe I could put in a good word for him." *More lies.*

Her brow puckered in thought and he waited, hoping for a lead that would give the narcs what they needed. Then he'd be out of it.

But she only shook her head. "I'll ask him when he comes in tonight."

"Don't bother," Brady said quickly. "I probably couldn't do anything anyway."

"Why don't we stay here tonight?" Anna suggested. "You're exhausted. I'll fix an omelette and toast and we can relax."

"You've been looking forward to the concert all week."

"I've been looking forward to being with you all week," she corrected gently. "Where we go doesn't matter. Don't you know that?"

"I'm beginning to," he murmured, and relaxed into the chair. "Tell me what's happening with you."

"Stephanie Wilkins actually read a paragraph today. The first time."

It helped.

He felt the tension drain from him as Anna's soft voice drifted over him. If only it were this simple all the time. The fading light touched her hair with a hint of gold. He'd close his eyes for a moment . . .

He woke to find Anna's hand on his shoulder.

"What?" He checked his watch. "How long have I been asleep?"

"An hour."

"An hour? Why didn't you wake me?"

She leaned over to touch her lips to his. "You looked like you needed the rest."

"I know something I need a lot more."

He glided his lips across hers and found softness, sweetness and . . . honesty.

He jerked to his feet. Honesty was the one thing he couldn't take from her, because he couldn't return it.

"I've got to go."

"Brady."

"I'll call you tomorrow. We'll do something. I'll make it up to you, I promise." He was babbling. He knew it. And he couldn't stop. He had to get out of there.

At home, he paid the baby-sitter. He looked at his reflection in the hallway mirror and doubted he'd be able to forgive himself anytime soon. Maybe never.

He slipped into Jennifer's room. By the muted glow of the nightlight, he gazed down at her. Gently, he pushed a strand of hair back from her face and touched his lips to her forehead. In Chad's room, he repeated the caress. In their faces he found a reason for what he was doing.

Getting drugs off the streets, making them

safe again for his kids — all kids — had to be his first priority. If he got hurt in the process, well, he'd known what he was getting into. He'd made his choices a long time ago.

But what of Anna? She hadn't made the choice; she hadn't even been asked.

The question gnawed at his conscience far into the night. Doing the right thing was scant consolation when it meant hurting the woman he loved.

Anna chewed on her lip as she looked at the phone. Brady hadn't been himself tonight. Though he'd denied it, she knew he was upset about something, but he'd seemed unable — or unwilling — to share it.

It hurt.

It hurt more than it ought to. It hurt, she acknowledged, because she loved him.

Picking up the receiver, she started to punch out his number. Just as quickly, she replaced it.

If Brady wanted to tell her what was wrong, he would. She'd given him plenty of openings. Just as it seemed he was about to open up, he'd changed the subject.

She looked at her lesson plans for the next day and pushed them aside as she noted the time. It was after eleven. Her body clamored for sleep but her mind still

198

wrestled with why Brady had shut her out. The only thing she could come up with was a problem at work that he couldn't discuss.

But, she argued with herself, if that was it, why hadn't he simply said so?

When Jeff came in, she was still on the couch.

"Waiting up?" he asked.

"No. I had something on my mind."

He slumped into a chair and laughed bitterly. "I thought you were onto a good thing, dating a cop, and all the while your boyfriend was playing you for a sucker."

She looked up. "What do you mean?"

"I mean he was using you. To get to me."

"You're wrong. Brady would never use me."

"If you don't believe me, ask him. Ask him if he's working with the narcs. They're after Mike and me. And you're their in."

"You're crazy."

"Am I?"

"Are you . . . using again?"

"I'm clean. For all the good it does me. No, big sister, it's not me who's crazy this time."

She looked at the boy — the man — who'd become a stranger to her, and felt she'd never known him. A piece of her died then.

"Go on. Ask him."

"How do you know all this?"

"Mike told me. He's got a source at the department. He also told me to tell you to keep your trap shut. Because when it goes down, he intends to be long gone."

"And you?"

"I'll be gone too."

Jeff was wrong. He had to be. Brady wouldn't — couldn't — use her. But then she remembered Brady's abstracted air, the questions about Jeff and Mike.

Around and around, her thoughts kept whirling, twirling, a kaleidoscope that shifted with every moment until she put her hands to her eyes to block out the pictures.

Anna wasn't surprised when Brady called the next day and asked if he could see her.

When he appeared that night, she schooled her expression to reveal none of what she was feeling. Right now, she didn't know *what* she was feeling besides a desperate need to have Jeff's accusation proven wrong.

"Hey, is something the matter?" Brady asked when she evaded his kiss.

"Why don't you tell me?"

He gave her a puzzled look. "I don't know —"

"Tell me about the new case." She watched as surprise, then understanding, registered on his face. In that moment, she knew Jeff hadn't lied. But because she wanted to be wrong, wanted it more than she'd ever wanted anything in her life, she waited, hoping.

"Are you working on a drug case?"

"Yes, but —"

"Are you investigating Jeff?"

His silence told her all she needed to know.

"And you decided to use me — our relationship — to find out what you wanted." The coldness of her voice was nothing compared to the iciness that surrounded her heart. "Is that why you brought Jennifer here in the first place? To get close to me, to Jeff?"

Now his voice was as cold as hers. "I'd never use Jennifer that way."

"No, I suppose not. Just me."

She'd struck home with that one. She could see it by the look on his face. But she didn't feel any triumph at her victory, only an infinite regret.

"Do you think I wanted to use you, Anna? Do you?" he demanded when she didn't answer.

"No. I don't think so. What I don't understand is why you did."

He turned to stare out the window. "Do you know how much drugs *come* into this city every year? Every week? Every day? Any schoolkid can lay his hands on crack." He wheeled around to face her once more. "Crack, Anna. Not just marijuana, but the hard stuff. I was assigned to find out anything I could to help put an end to it."

"Using whatever means you could."

He returned her gaze without flinching. "Using whatever means I could."

"Even if it meant using me?" She watched as his face paled.

"Yes," he said evenly. "Even if it meant using you."

She respected his honesty, even though it hurt. She wanted to hate him but found she couldn't. He hadn't tried to spare himself. He could have easily lied, and she'd have believed him because she wanted to, wanted to more than she'd ever wanted anything.

"I never wanted to hurt *you*, Anna. You don't have to believe that, but it's the truth."

"Sorry, I can't make that distinction."

"I'm sorry," he said, pulling her to him.

She shrank from his touch and pushed him away. "I was worried that I was using you, and all the time you were using me, trying to find out about Jeff."

"Not all the time," he said softly. "Everything I said to you was the truth, Anna. I love you."

Words she'd longed to hear only a day ago were now meaningless.

"You must have thought I was a real dope. No wonder you didn't mind helping me find Jeff. You needed him for your drug bust. What were you going to do? Track him down and then arrest him?"

"Yes, I needed him. And I might have had to arrest him. But that wasn't why I helped you find him."

"Yeah?" Her gaze raked over him contemptuously. "Pull the other one, detective."

"I helped you because I love you, because I care what happens to you. And to Jeff."

"Love? You don't even know the meaning of the word."

The spasm of pain that crossed his face shamed her even as she said words she knew weren't true. Brady had a great capacity for love. He'd shown that with Jennifer and Chad.

"That's where you're wrong." He drew her to him to settle a kiss upon her lips.

Insistent and demanding, the kiss could not be ignored. Against her will, she felt herself responding to it . . . to him. At last she pushed away from him and wiped her mouth, anger and pain making her want to strike back.

"You have a funny way of showing it. Is this how you treat all your snitches? Or just me?"

"I've never said that to another woman."

For the first time, she wondered if she'd been wrong. She looked at him and winced at the lines of pain she saw etched on his face. New lines scored his forehead, while grooves were carved around his mouth. His eyes looked old. Like they'd seen too much and cared too much.

Angry at herself for wanting to believe him, she turned away. He was still using her, just as he had before. Only this time she wasn't falling for it.

"You got what you wanted. Just leave us alone."

"What I want is . . . It doesn't matter what I want. What matters right now is Jeff. He needs help, Anna."

"Sure, detective, I know how much you care about my brother. Well, Jeff's fine. No thanks to you."

He grabbed her arm. "Stop lying, Anna.

If not to me, then at least to yourself. Jeff's in trouble, and you know it."

She jerked away from him. "What's it to you if he is?"

"I care about him. And about you." He cupped her chin, forcing her to look at him. "Even if you don't believe anything else, you have to know I'd never deliberately hurt you."

"I don't know what I believe anymore," she said weakly, her anger spent. She felt him staring at her, knowing he wanted to say something more. She didn't have the strength to hear it now.

Please leave, she begged silently.

He must have understood her unspoken plea for, after giving her one last look, he let himself quietly out the door.

More tired than she'd ever been, she dropped onto the sofa and tried not to feel. If she could turn off her feelings, maybe she could survive the night.

She didn't dare think beyond tonight.

She tried to convince herself that whatever she felt for Brady had died when she'd learned of his deception. Her mind understood, but her heart refused to accept the lie.

He was still Brady. The man she loved.

CHAPTER ELEVEN

"Sis, can we talk?"

Anna couldn't hide her surprise at Jeff's words. "Sure. What about?"

"I've been a jerk the last six months. I blamed you, Mom, everyone but myself." He laughed without humor. "I really screwed up."

"What can I do?" she asked cautiously.

"Nothing. This is something I've got to do on my own. I just wanted you to know, however this turns out, I'm sorry."

She stood, reaching up to hug him. "I'm sorry too, Jeff. We've both made mistakes. But it's not too late."

"I hope not," he said so softly that she had to strain to catch the words. "I've got to go out. I've got some business to take care of."

"But —"

"If I'm lucky, I'll be out of this." He gave her a peck on the cheek. "Wish me luck."

"Jeff, wait," she called, but he was already out the door.

She stared after him. How long had it been since Jeff had kissed her? She touched her cheek. She wasn't surprised to find it wet with tears.

Three hours later, she was frantic. There'd been no word from Jeff. She checked his room. Despite her worry, she smiled as she picked her way over the clutter of clothes, shoes, and sports equipment. Some things never changed.

Her smile died as she started looking for something — anything — that would give her a clue as to where Jeff went. She was about to give up when she spotted the scrap of paper, its edge sticking out from beneath the desk blotter. Two words were scrawled across it: bus station.

She studied it. There was no way to determine when it had been written. But it was all she had. She grabbed her purse when the doorbell rang. Impatiently, she jerked open the door to find Brady standing there.

"Sorry," she said. "I'm on my way out."

He grabbed her arm. "Where?"

"Out." She tried to free her arm, but he held it fast and led her back into the living room.

"Where's Jeff?"

"Why do you want to know?"

"I don't have time for games, Anna."

He rubbed his hand across his face, drawing her attention to the day-old stubble that darkened his jaw. His eyes were bloodshot, his suit rumpled.

"Where's Jeff?" he repeated.

"What do you want now, Detective Matthews? More information?"

Her words lashed him like the sting of a whip. He wanted to haul her into his arms and kiss away the bitterness he saw in her eyes, but he didn't have time for personal feelings now.

If the information they'd received at the precinct was correct, Jeff's life was at stake. And the lives of a lot of other kids if that dope reached the street.

"I don't blame you for being angry. But that's not going to do Jeff any good."

"What do you care about Jeff? Except to use him to make your precious case."

"If you really believe that then we have nothing left to talk about. The question is: do you believe it?"

"No," she said quietly. "I don't believe it."

"Good."

He couldn't quite hide the satisfaction her words gave him. If she believed that he cared about Jeff, maybe there was still hope for a future for them. But he couldn't think of that now. Right now, Jeff needed them. And Brady was very much afraid that time was running out.

He gripped her shoulders. "This is serious. It's not kid stuff anymore. Jeff's in trouble. More trouble than he realizes. More trouble than you realize."

He watched her face blanch. *Good.* He'd wanted to shock her. Maybe now she'd tell him what he needed to know to help her brother.

"Now, where is he?"

"Who's asking? Brady Matthews the friend? Or Detective Matthews the cop?"

"Both." He sighed heavily. "Anna, I can't help you if you won't let me." He checked his watch. "If you care about your brother, you'll tell me where he is."

"Of course I care about my brother. That's where I'm . . ." Her words hung in the air.

"Then you do know where he is. For Jeff's sake, tell me. If you care about him at all, tell me." He saw the indecision in her eyes, the doubt, the fear. He only prayed she'd trust him enough to tell him the truth.

"He's at the old bus station. He said he had something he had to take care of and then he'd be out of it."

"Honey, don't you see? People like that won't let Jeff walk away. I've got to get to him."

"I'm going with you."

He grazed her cheek with his knuckles. "I can't let you do that. It's against department regulations. And if anything happened to you, I'd never forgive myself."

"Either I go with you or I go by myself. Your choice."

Brady weighed the options. He didn't have any choice, short of handcuffing her to a chair. At the moment, that didn't seem a half bad idea.

"We're wasting time," she reminded him.

He tried one more time. "It's not safe. I can't help Jeff if I'm watching out for you."

"Brady, I have to go. Please."

The plea in her voice chipped away at his resolve. A demand he could have withstood, but the soft entreaty undermined all his arguments.

"Come on."

Inside the squad car, he made sure she was buckled into the seat belt, then strapped himself in.

He called for backup on the radio and muttered something under his breath when it blared back a message. He glanced at

Anna's face and saw she didn't understand the significance of what she'd just heard — the code for a hostage situation. He prayed she never would.

"Jeff's all I have," she whispered. "If something happens to him . . ."

"I won't let anything happen to him," Brady said, and prayed he could make good on the promise.

Lights flashing and siren blaring, the patrol car wove through traffic.

Brady glanced at Anna. Her eyes, dark with fear, looked too big for her face, reminding him of the first time he'd seen her. He wanted to take her hand, cradle it within his own. But for Jeff's sake, as well as hers, he needed to keep his mind clear.

He'd have done anything to spare her this. Then he wondered if that were true. He'd told her the truth when he said he'd have used what she'd told him if it would have helped to get a lead on the drug operation.

Maybe if he pushed harder. He shook his head, impatient with his indecision. Second-guessing wouldn't help Jeff now. Brady pushed away his doubts. He'd done what he'd had to.

Anna gripped his arm. "Can't we go any faster?"

"We're going too fast already. We'll make it." He just prayed they'd make it in time.

"Do you . . . do you think he's all right?"

Brady knew what it had cost her to ask that question. He resisted the urge to look at her and forced a reassuring nod, even though he wasn't sure of anything but his need to comfort her.

The scene at the bus station was a cop's worst nightmare. Patrol cars surrounded the building. Brady could see Mike Rafferty with an arm wrapped around Jeff's neck, the glint of a knife barely visible. The bulge under Rafferty's jacket was unmistakably a gun.

He turned to Anna. Her face was pale under the moonlight. "Stay here."

"Jeff's out there."

"Anna, I can't take care of you and help Jeff at the same time."

He reached out to touch her cheek, to reassure her that everything was going to be all right, but then dropped his hand. He contented himself with squeezing her shoulder.

Rafferty, using Jeff as a shield, started toward a van parked just outside the perimeter of police cars.

Brady watched their progress. The breath hissed between his teeth as he saw

Rafferty press the knife against Jeff's throat when a patrolman advanced too close.

Brady glanced at Anna, hoping she didn't see the knife. One look at her face told him she had.

"I have to —" she began.

"Stay here," he growled. He rolled onto the ground, keeping to the shadows. He had begun crawling on his belly when he saw Anna start to follow him.

"Anna, no!"

But she'd already run ahead of him. "Jeff! Jeff!"

Common sense warned him to stay where he was. But he couldn't let Anna run into an armed Rafferty. Brady broke cover and ran toward her, knocking her down and shielding her with his own body. He hadn't realized he was holding his breath until he heard the whoosh of air.

The breath knocked from her, Anna tried to breathe. Brady was covering her, and she pushed against his chest.

He caught her hands and clamped them together.

"Stay here," he said. "I mean it," he added when she tried to wriggle out from under him.

Bedlam broke loose as shots were exchanged. Brady trained his gaze toward where he'd last seen Rafferty and Jeff. Rafferty was nowhere to be seen, but Jeff lay crumpled on the ground.

Cautiously, Brady made his way to Jeff. He felt for a pulse and found one.

He cursed softly when he felt Anna beside him. "I told you to stay put."

"He's my brother." She knelt beside Jeff and touched his temple. A warm stickiness matted his hair. "Jeff!" She shook him. "Please . . ."

Brady pried her away. "Anna, he'll be all right. You can't help him right now. The paramedics will look after him."

She clung to her brother until Brady forcibly pulled her away.

"You did this," she said, her voice shrill. "You did this. If Jeff . . . it'll be your fault. You promised you'd protect him. You lied to me. You lied."

The venom in her voice sluiced over him.

Before he could answer, paramedics were pushing them out of the way. He watched helplessly as they worked on Jeff before putting him on a stretcher. Anna followed them to an ambulance. He started to go with her when she turned on him.

The look in her eyes alone was enough

to make him stop. But her words made certain of it. "Don't."

He watched as she stumbled over the rough ground, aching to take her in his arms.

You lied.

The words echoed through his mind, taunting him until he clamped his hands over his ears in an effort to block out the accusation.

He felt as though he'd been kicked in the gut. He longed to go to Anna and make her understand. Instead, he turned his attention to the mopping up that had to be done.

Handcuffed, Rafferty no longer looked menacing. He looked like what he was — a street punk on his way to jail. When he got out, Brady thought with satisfaction, Rafferty would no longer be young. He'd be pushing middle age.

At the station, Brady looked around. The normality of the scene was a welcome counterpoint to the madness he'd just left. He savored the clatter of the typewriter, the shrill of the telephone, the good-natured bantering among the night shift. And because it was all so normal, he let himself believe that the last hour was only a nightmare, that he could wake up and blink it away.

But the blood on his shirt made a lie of that fantasy. Jeff's blood. Brady hadn't noticed it until now. It had come from Anna's hands when she'd grabbed his shirt.

His own hands shook as he realized it could just as easily have been Anna's blood that now stained his shirt. His face blanched at the thought.

He flinched inwardly as he recalled the accusations she'd hurled at him. That he deserved all that and more didn't lessen the pain. That she'd refused to let him come to the hospital with her only magnified his guilt.

He'd made a promise to her, and he'd broken it. Even if Anna forgave him, he didn't believe he'd ever be able to forgive himself.

In her bedroom, Anna peeled off her clothes. They smelled of cigarettes and stale coffee, thanks to her vigil at the hospital.

Outside, the wind sobbed its cry, a soulful moan that echoed the ache in her heart. She closed the window, but the plaintive cry of the wind penetrated the glass barrier.

Jeff was going to be all right. The bullet had creased his temple, resulting in a lot of blood but no permanent damage. She held on to that fact and concentrated on blocking out everything else.

Forgiveness didn't come easily, she acknowledged. She'd let Jeff down with her tunnel vision. If she'd admitted that he had a problem weeks — months — ago, maybe he wouldn't be lying in the hospital now.

But it wasn't Jeff's face she was seeing. It was Brady's.

The enormity of what she'd done haunted her as she remembered the ugly accusations she'd hurled at him.

"Brady, what have I done?"

Her whisper went unanswered as it drifted into the night. The wind had subsided, whimpering pitifully. She tried not to listen to the mournful sob; it reminded her too much of the cry in her heart.

When pain and guilt had exacted their price, she slept. But sleep didn't ease the guilt. It only postponed it.

Each time the phone rang, she hoped. And when hope frayed, she prayed. When she could bear the uncertainty and loneliness no longer, she called him.

"Brady?"

"Yeah?"

Impatience edged his voice, and she

hesitated. "It's me . . . Anna."

"Are you all right?"

"I'm fine."

"That's good."

The remoteness in his voice hurt her.

What had she expected? She'd ordered him out of her life. Her face burned as she remembered the accusations she'd flung at him. He probably hated her. She could scarcely blame him. She'd accused him of using her when all he'd been trying to do was protect Jeff and all the other kids like him by getting drugs off the street.

"Uh . . . I just wanted to let you know that Jeff's going to be all right. He's in a treatment center now."

His voice warmed. "That's great news."

"I think he's going to be all right. I just thought I'd tell you."

"Thanks for calling."

She waited, hoping he'd say something else, something more personal, but he didn't. She recradled the phone, feeling more desolate than ever. He couldn't have made it plainer that he was no longer interested.

Hot July days dragged into August. Jeff was making progress. The doctors warned her to not expect too much too soon, but she couldn't help feeling that everything would be all right, She would get her brother back. He'd still have to stand trial, but they'd cross that hurdle when they came to it.

Together they'd start building a new relationship, a healthy one that didn't dwell on the past. This time, Anna resolved, she wasn't going to play the role of Jeff's mother. Those days were over. She was his sister. Period.

A smile curved her lips. She found she was looking forward to a new start with her brother.

Meanwhile, her students kept her sane. Encouraging them, praising them, and, occasionally, prodding them, took her out of herself, forcing her to think of someone other than Brady and what she had lost. They were frequently funny, occasionally rude, and infinitely dear because they were hers.

She thanked heaven for them.

Late one afternoon, eight-year-old Sammy Paulson pushed his chair back from the table, nearly knocking her over.

"Miss Lancaster, I can read. I can read it! I can read the words. They're not mixed up anymore."

The little boy danced in excitement.

Anna grabbed him and twirled him

around. "I knew you could do it."

"We found the missing piece, didn't we?" he asked.

"We . . ." Her voice failed, and she tried again. "We sure did, Sammy."

When his mother picked him up and learned the news, she cried unashamedly. She pressed Anna's hand. "Thank you."

Tears pricked Anna's own eyes, tears she didn't bother to wipe away. She could see a rent in the grayness that had colored her life for the last weeks, a slice of light that told her she was still alive.

She was starting to heal.

She didn't kid herself. Life without Brady promised to be a lonely proposition. But she was a survivor. She had Jeff and her students. They were enough.

They had to be.

CHAPTER TWELVE

Brady had stopped hoping that Anna would call. It was over. He'd better learn to live with it or he'd go crazy. If he wasn't already crazy, that is. Right now, he wasn't sure.

Except for that one brief call she'd made to tell him that Jeff was going to be all right, there'd been nothing. He'd already checked on Jeff, relieved to learn that the wound was superficial. He'd made a couple of calls to the district attorney and the public defender and learned that Jeff would probably get a reduced sentence in return for testifying against Rafferty when his trial came up.

So her call had been an anticlimax. He'd waited, hoped, prayed, for something more. But her voice had been strained, her tone that of someone talking to a stranger.

That was what hurt most of all.

Brady looked at his desk, for once grateful for the paperwork that covered its surface. Filling out reports would keep him too busy to think of Anna. He picked up a form and rolled it into the typewriter. His fingers punched the keys with more determination than accuracy.

The arrest of Mike Rafferty and the rest of his fellow drug dealers had gone a long way toward cleaning up the streets. They'd found Rafferty's source in the department — a stenographer in the detectives' division.

Brady wasn't naive enough to think that Rafferty's arrest was the end of it. There'd be another pusher, preying on the weak, the unknowing, the innocent. At one time, Brady would have been depressed by the realization. But not now.

Anna had made the difference. She'd made him see that what he did mattered. If he couldn't right all the world's wrongs, he could do his best to help this one small corner of the world. And, by doing so, he'd found the satisfaction he'd been missing in his job. Anna would've been pleased.

A faint smile lifted the corners of his mouth as he realized his thoughts had gone full circle, as always, bringing him back to Anna.

Would he ever stop missing her, ever stop wanting her, ever stop loving her? The answer came swiftly and painfully.

No.

Anna pulled her belt one notch tighter. She'd lost weight during the last month. The mirror confirmed it, and she grimaced at the hollows carved into her cheeks.

When the phone rang, she couldn't help the small thread of hope that wove its way through her. Despite everything, that speck of hope refused to die. Eagerly, she picked up the phone, then braced herself for the inevitable pain when she realized it wasn't Brady.

"Anna?"

"Yes?"

"It's Jennifer." The girlish voice sounded more grown-up than Anna remembered.

The thought gave her a momentary pang, which she pushed away. Jennifer wasn't a part of her life any longer.

"Is something wrong? Are you and Chad all right?"

"We're fine," Jennifer said. "It's Uncle Brady."

"Brady? Is he sick? Did something happen to him at work? Was he hurt?" The questions came before she could stop them.

"Not exactly," Jennifer said.

Were those sniffles?

"What exactly then?" Anna asked, trying hard to keep her voice calm.

"Could you come over?"

She didn't have to think about it. "I'll be there in ten minutes."

She made it in eight.

"What is it?" she asked after Jennifer led her into the kitchen.

"I miss you."

Anna hugged the little girl. "I miss you too, honey. You and Chad both. Are you still working on your reading?"

For the first time, Jennifer smiled. "My new teacher's nice, but not as nice as you. By the time school starts, I'll be reading anything I want." Her smile vanished. "Anna, are you mad at Uncle Brady because of me?"

"Because of . . . No, Jennifer, I'm not mad because of you. We settled all that, remember?"

"But you are mad at him, aren't you?"

"I was once. But not anymore. Your uncle is a very brave man. He's also a very good man. Is he . . ." Anna swallowed and tried again. "Is he all right?"

Jennifer appeared to think that over. "He doesn't talk much, and he hardly ever kids around with us like he used to. He *looks* all right. On the outside."

Looks all right on the outside. What did that mean?

"But he's sad on the inside."

"How do you know?"

"He hurts here." Jennifer placed a hand over her heart. "Uncle Brady said you made him happy. Won't you do it again?"

The simple gesture touched Anna more than she cared to admit. Her own heart echoed that pain. Was it possible Brady missed her as much as she missed him? Hope flared briefly until she remembered the horrible things she'd accused him of. Even if he did miss her, he couldn't possibly forgive her.

Could he?

Jennifer's words drew Anna back. "I wish you'd come back, Anna. I'm sorry about all the things I said before. Chad and me both miss you. Uncle Brady does too. But he doesn't let on."

"How do you know he misses me?"

"Because he looks sad all the time. He didn't even yell when Chad put honey on the toilet seat."

Anna suppressed a smile. "That is serious."

"Will you talk with him and help him feel better?" Jennifer asked. "Chad and me do our best, but it's not the same."

Anna hesitated. "It's not that simple. Your uncle and I . . . we . . ."

"Did you have a fight?"

"No. But we did have a disagreement and said things that hurt each other."

"Uncle Brady says if you're mad at someone, you should go to him and tell him why and then make up. He always makes Chad and me make up before we go to bed if we've had a fight."

"That's good advice, but I don't know if it'll work with us."

"Why not?"

"Because, we're grown up and sometimes things don't work like they should."

"You mean you and Uncle Brady can't make up because you're grown-ups?"

Put that way it sounded ridiculous, and Anna wondered how a nine-year-old girl had become so wise. She, in turn, felt more mixed up than ever.

"So, are you going to make up with Uncle Brady?" Jennifer persisted.

"It looks like I don't have any choice," Anna said, feeling happier than she had in weeks. She tried to tamp down the hope Jennifer's words had given her, but she couldn't help the surge of energy that flowed through her at the thought of seeing Brady again.

If Jennifer were right . . . If Brady really did miss her . . . If he could forgive what she'd said to him . . . Twenty minutes later her courage fled as she walked into the precinct station.

The air smelled of coffee and stale smoke, reminding her of her first visit there.

After asking where she could find Brady, she made her way to the squad room. She saw him, hunched over a desk and looking achingly tired. Guilt washed over her as she realized she bore at least part of the blame for the new lines that bracketed his mouth and fanned from the corners of his eyes.

Brady looked up. "Anna."

She tried a smile and found it more difficult than she'd imagined. "How are you?"

He gestured to the files scattered across his desk. "Swamped."

"If I'm interrupting . . ."

"No. You're not, but we can't talk here." He stood and ushered her into the lunch room, where he pulled out a chair for her.

Anna sat down and looked around, stalling for time. Vending machines lined gunmetal gray walls. Linoleum that might once have been green, now dulled to a muddy brown, covered the floor. A table, its top worn smooth by the years, occupied the center of the room.

"I didn't know if you'd see me," she said

at last. "I wouldn't blame you if you didn't want to."

He didn't pretend to misunderstand. "I always want to see you, Anna. Don't you know that?"

Her smile trembled around the edges but remained in place. "I was hoping. After the way I treated you . . . the things I said . . ."

"You were hurting."

"That doesn't excuse what I said to you. You were only trying to help. If you hadn't pushed me to the ground I'd probably be —"

"Don't." His face whitened. "Don't say that."

"But it's true," she insisted. "You saved my life. Just as you saved Jeff's. If I'd told you where he was sooner, maybe he wouldn't be . . ."

He put his hands on her shoulders. "Quit blaming yourself. You were trying to protect your brother. Anyone would have done the same thing."

"I should've known you wouldn't hurt Jeff — or me. I was just so scared."

He hitched a hip onto the table. "I know. It's over now."

"Not yet. Jeff's agreed to stay at the treatment center. I think he means it this time."

"I'm glad."

"He'll still have to stand trial. But his lawyer said he'll probably get a reduced sentence since he's agreed to testify against Rafferty and the others."

Her eyes filled with tears. "Maybe someday you'll get to meet him — the *real* Jeff, I mean. He was a good kid. I know he can be again."

"If he's anything like his sister, he'd have to be." Brady checked his watch. "If that's all . . ."

He's decided not to forgive me. She couldn't blame him. She fought back the tears and pushed the chair away from the table.

"Anna?"

"What?"

"Was there something else?"

"No." *Only that I love you.*

"I thought maybe . . ."

Hope surged through her as she waited.

"Jennifer and Chad really miss you. If you're not too busy, maybe you could stop by to see them."

"Oh." Disappointment chased away the hope. "I'd be glad to."

"Anna?" He paused. "They're not the only ones who miss you."

"They aren't?"

"I miss you too."

The simple statement caused her steps

to falter, her heartbeat to stammer at an uneven pace. She dared to turn and look at him. "You do?"

"Don't you know that?"

Afraid to trust her voice, she shook her head.

"It's true. I miss you so much that I ache with it. Most of all, I need you. I need you to chase away the loneliness." He laughed shortly. "I didn't even know I was lonely until I met you. I want to share the bad times with you as well as the good. I want to go to bed with you at night and wake up with you in the morning. I need you to make it . . ." he gestured around him, ". . . all worthwhile."

"I need you too," she whispered. The love she saw in his eyes couldn't be mistaken for anything else.

As if to prove it, he said, "I love you. I have for a long time."

"I didn't know. After all that happened, I wasn't sure."

"We've both made mistakes. That's what love's about — making mistakes and then forgiving each other."

"I said terrible things to you."

He didn't deny it. "It doesn't matter. If you love me, nothing else matters. Do you, Anna? Do you love me?"

Too overcome to speak, she could only nod.

"I love you," Brady repeated. "If you'll have me, I intend to spend the rest of my life proving it to you."

"You already have."

He pulled her down to his lap and closed his mouth over hers.

"Hey, Matthews . . ." Davies burst in, took in the situation, and grinned. "I'll tell the lieutenant you're interviewing a witness and can't be disturbed."

I should be embarrassed, Anna thought. But she couldn't bring herself to feel upset. She was too happy.

Brady nuzzled Anna's neck. "It's official now. Caught kissing in the lunch room. You'll have to marry me to salvage my reputation."

"Is that the only reason I should marry you?" she asked, lifting her head so that their lips met.

"Well, I can think of a few others," he said and proceeded to show her.

The employees of Thorndike Press hope you have enjoyed this Large Print book. All our Thorndike and Wheeler Large Print titles are designed for easy reading, and all our books are made to last. Other Thorndike Press Large Print books are available at your library, through selected bookstores, or directly from us.

For information about titles, please call:

(800) 223-1244

or visit our Web site at:

www.gale.com/thorndike
www.gale.com/wheeler

To share your comments, please write:

Publisher
Thorndike Press
295 Kennedy Memorial Drive
Waterville, ME   04901